MW01362225

gerbil møther

NeWest Press

gerbil møther

D.M. Bryan

Library and Archives Canada Cataloguing in Publication

Bryan, Dawn M., 1964–
Gerbil mother / D.M. Bryan.
(Nunatak fiction)

ISBN 978-1-897126-24-0

I. Title. II. Series.

PS8603.R887G47 2008 C813'.6 C2007-906072-2

Editor for the Board: Suzette Mayr
Cover and interior design: Natalie Olsen
Author photo: L.E. Bryan

Canada Council for the Arts Conseil des Arts du Canada

Canadian Heritage Patrimoine canadien

NeWest Press acknowledges the support of the Canada Council for the Arts, the Alberta Foundation for the Arts, and the Edmonton Arts Council for our publishing program. We also acknowledge the financial support of the Government of Canada through the Book Publishing Industry Development Program (BPIDP).

NeWest Press
#201 8540.109 Street
Edmonton, Alberta t6g 1e6
780.432.9427
newestpress.com

No bison were harmed in the making of this book.
We are committed to protecting the environment and to the responsible use of natural resources. This book is printed on 100% recycled, ancient forest-friendly paper.

1 2 3 4 5 11 10 09 08

printed and bound in Canada

før Richard, Jøel, and Aphra

TAKE IT ON TRUST — the moment's a bad one. Not Greek tragedy, but ordinary doctor's office despair, regular as a diagrammed digestive system.

Wherever I happen to look in the doctor's tiny office, I see pin-ups of major body functions. Over the desk hang the Skeletal, Muscular, and Lymphatic systems. Above the black examining table someone has pinned Endocrine, Cardiovascular, Urinary, and Nervous, all in a staggered row. Next to the open door where my chart waits in its plastic holder, Digestion dangles by a single tack. I study the drawing's purple mounds and pinkish loops, naming body parts in a wash of liquid sound: esophagus, epiglottis, colon, appendix. I mouth the words and taste the blood, tongue the trachea, lick the liver. And because this new moment is as bad as the one before, I suffer confusion over insides and outsides. My stomach twists into lips, grows teeth, starts chewing.

Take it on trust — another moment like the other moments will scarf me down, will grind me up. And that's fine with me — maybe I *want* to vanish.

I wait. Something sticks in my craw.

GACK.

Hang on. Got a lung I need to cough up. Hawk and spit. Give me just a second; don't you wander off. You'll want to be here as I wipe liquid from my almond eyes, sneeze fluid from my twitchy nose. With fingers (paws, really), I smooth back hair and pat strands into place. Tuck in my famous tail. Prodigious me. Incomparable Gerbil.

Look at me now, huh? I'm feeling better. I'm better than better. Take it from me — the moment's a good one. Let me draw us a picture. Lift your hands. Sure, I mean those hands. Now place them on your sternum — found it? Good. Next, describe me an arc, a big curve in the air, an inflatable stadium or a cathedral's dome. Rest your hands on your mons pubis because that's where we stop. Edge of my roof. Roof of my house. That's where we start: my motherland, an architecture filled with nothing. Now I'm drawing us a ceiling, a vaulted orange skin, hallways ribbed with whistling breath, parquet of heartbeats syncopated with the tick-tock of my own sunken chest. Cornices, flaking baseboards, trickling closets suggesting damp, a basement that sloshes, that drains, that fills again with the rushing of water. My house. My home.

My mother.

Full of chew holes, she is. A draining away to my rising tide. Look. Waters churn and dribble from my furry ears. Fluid in my lungs, in my mouth, but here's my voice — shrill and peeping, with things to say. I call out. I call out, and for an instant my mother seems to answer. Listen. This is what she says.

— Yes?

But in the moment it's already clear she's talking to someone else. She is. Yes.

— Huh?

— Did you say?...

chapter øne

— I thought you said ...

— No.

Another flood — plus offstage rustling. Distant voices. Who's that? What's going on? If we were a story we'd be a potboiler. This story all wet behind the ears.

— What?

Are you talking to me?

My mother speaks again. Yes. What. Man. She said. Not sure.

Somewhere a chair creaks. Someone intones sets of coordinates. Jelly. Paddle.

Outside, certain operations, certain medical procedures, progress. Inside, the waters lap. A whale song lulls me with its subsonic lullaby, its cradle song of ultrasound echoes. The music goes on and on, describing me to a T in a descant of vertebrae, of tendons plucked. A score of limbs transcribed and weighed. The deep, deep tremolo of organs. That bloody refrain: occipital, transverse, anterior.

After a time the underwater music stops.

Into the silence my mother speaks. — You can't tell me anything, I know.

Another voice, calm and professional, agrees.

My mother has sailed into deep waters, chartless and dark. Her fear produces no sounding, only echoes, only amplifications of itself.

Then into ocean depths, the voice again, a little rushed now, strictly unofficial. — But I see nothing for you to worry about, says the voice. — Nothing.

— It's just that I was lucky the first time, and now I can't help —

— I know. Don't worry.

My mother breathes. — Can I see? she says.

I hear the swivel of an off-screen screen. — Can you take a picture?

— Not much there yet.

— But still?

— There's a nominal charge.

— Man?

The shell burst of light shocks me — the single strobe, the flash pot. My first photo call, a star already. I shut my eyes — no time to pose — the afterimage already forming under my lids, developing before my eyes. First, a whiteness, then a network of shadows that doubles, spreads, divides, doubles again. And then a clearing in the brainpan, the onrush of outside: salt of handled steel, chew of vinyl, leak of urine. Listen to the rustle of the ultrasound photograph in my mother's hand. Inside that Polaroid's white boundaries lurks a printed monster: brain-bloated, grain-limbed, spine-dashed, eye-socked, fetal-curved, digit-less, tailed, eared, whiskered. Gerbil. Me.

∅

Later, my mother floats in her own tub full of water. She soaks in darkness, liquid behind lids. Floating and soaking begin a list of things we have in common, including her eyes, orbs moistened in saline, sore with looking, her fingers, her toes so very countable, and inside her, in a gilt frame over a mantelpiece of marble, my Polaroid photograph.

I've learned to live with that slick mirror, but already I'm changing.

For example, I'm tired of being at sea. I wish I had a fire in the grate; I wish I had a rocking chair; I wish I had a braided rug, a crocheted throw, a pillow embroidered with "Home Sweet Home." But, then, this story hides no Aladdin's lamp. This story stars no teeny genie. This story has a rock for a heart but floats like pumice.

As for me, I'm treading water — catching my breath, having a think. There's a warm wash up to my mother's waterline, but she's waxed and cold above deck. If she were a boat, I guess I'd be in her cabin, or maybe the cockpit, or maybe below deck in steerage. If she were a boat, I wouldn't be swimming. I might be drier, not dreaming of gills, of little webbed fingers, of duck feet. I'd go up on deck to waddle under stars, to get a little peace, a little quiet. But my mother's no boat, just adrift in a bathtub. She's a stretched-out bag of bones in soapy water and baked earth, floating and watching my elbow, my knees, as I bang, and kick, and turn, and churn the water inside her.

Be warned, our mothership–Gerbil communion ends here — all illusion, anyway, given the divided moment that made it possible. From this point on, a third party crashes our party, arriving as a distant screech that pops the membrane of sudsy water and pierces our twin menisci. Two sets of soaking bones, one hard and one soft, are set a-roiling in our paired tubs, until some accord stretched between us pulls rottenly apart as if immersed too long below the waterline. My motherland lifts her head, looks away from my phenomenal, my show-stopping acrobatics. Gazes at butter yellow wall, white tile, at steamy mirror, at window blue and snow rimmed. She listens to a voice, a shrieking set of phonemes that could never come from me. To make sure, I open and close my own mouth, but shrieks demonstrate independence from my lips, my larynx. A mind of its own demands hurtles through the doorway.

— Nick. She names the shrieker, seems to know him well. My mother turns her head and waits for him to appear. Here he comes, skidding to a stop, crouching down beside the tub. Eyes blue, teeth white, and tonsils red. — Nicky. Nicholas. Nick!

(Forgotten in the dark, I'm treading water, eyes wide open, annoyed. Don't like this shrieking; don't like this shrieker.)

— What's the matter. Nicky sweetheart?

The shrieker gibbers, wails — his cries untranslatable, unmistakable.

— Tell Mommy.

A rising tide of howls.

My mother's voice attempts reasonableness, achieves only panic.

— Nick, use your words!

Wild notes, graceless notes, distressed footnotes slip to the bathroom tiles.

— Don't, Nick.

But he shrieks like a proverbial fingernail on that board of deep-sea green.

I keep treading water, and then I touch bottom, tippy-toes in muck suddenly firm footed. And in that yellowed well of a bathroom, my mother hits bottom too, half rises from the water. Suds slosh against tub walls, against my walls, and I rise with her. The porcelain feels cool under hands, but here comes hot anger: rushing wind through an opened valve. We inflate until all puffed up. Floating under the ceiling, an evil balloon — we go off with a bang. Nick cowers on the lino. He shrinks down, stops screaming, lets her deflate all over him.

Oh, I see at once what a bad mother we have. Yes I do.

But she says: Shhh, shhh. Nickie-Nick. I'm sorry sweetie-pie. Shhh.

∅

My room invites me to bed. Now there's a four-poster smack dab in the centre of my room — pillows heaped, the sheet turned back just for me. True, I'm tired, tired from my first day. Been a long day, and I'm only small yet. Think of me now, measurable in Lilliputian inches, swimming toward my flannel blankets. Outside and around me, my mother dries herself, dries my brother, sadly lifts him over her shoulder, carries him to bed. We lack a candle to blow out with a gentle puff. Her finger on the light switch will have to do. Nick has a blue room, just darkened. He has a barred crib with a comforter that fails to comfort. On my mother's shoulder he drooped, heavy lids reefed, but now Nick stands bolt upright in bed, perpendicular with fresh rage. He shakes the railing of his crib — drawing anger from a deep, deep well. Calling: Hey 'erbil. Com' on 'erbil.

Against his red face flushed with anger, my mother whimpers, shuts the door. Nick will cry himself to sleep. So, too, in her big bed, will my swampy motherland. Me? I've got my mouth open in astonishment, my almond eyes dry and wide. Caught. Red-handed. How did he know I was here?

No sleep tonight for Gerbil. For 'erbil. Not a wink.

ø

I must lie awake and contemplate the following koan: how does Nicholas know my name?

Dumb luck?

He could have called for Rabbit. Or Mole. A kid like him might have chosen Ferret or Mousie or Stoat. Random selection might throw out Woodbug. Or Tick. Tapeworm is good — a certain interiority in common there. Or if he must guess a rodent, why not a rat? Rats have been rehabilitated — now understood to be intelligent and personable. Cute even. These days everyone wants a rat in a cage, or tucked in a pocket eating crackers. Rat. Ratty. 'Atty.

And Nick, now that I come to think things over, how has Gerbil even come to be one of your words? You have so few; they serve you so poorly. What random image from television caught on the sticky flypaper of your intelligence? No other gerbil lives in this apartment or I would know. While I toss and turn, considering your riddle in this dark of darks, my mother sleeps on, innocent of urine sodden bedding, of overpriced feeds, of the greenish water bottle and the futile wheel. She knows nothing of Gerbils. What do you know, brother Nicholas?

My brother makes me no answer, only slumbers on in the room next door.

I cross to the desk, rest elbows on time-tinted oak, place head in paws. I must do some serious thinking about Nick, and the task pleases me not.

The time has come to confront the following certainties: I'm living in Nick's old place. His desk, his bed, his braided throw. The wallpaper I thought was new this morning — he knew this wallpaper. Perhaps he picked it out himself. I step back, take a better look at my surroundings, newly suspicious of cranium-shaped recesses, frayed edges, shiny spots. I sniff for the stink of bachelor brother, hunt for balled up sweat socks, stained y-fronts. I grope with doubting paws, poke with inquisitive nose but find nothing beyond a slyly hinting stretchiness to everything around me — a taint of ghost mould in the shape of the walls. If I pressed modelling clay against those dents over there what would I discover? The set of Nick's brow? The line of his cheek? The print of his teeth?

Primogeniture. It starts with the pre-chewed tit and cuts to the second hand bike. Nothing for certain, but the answer to Nick's koan is this: my brother bears watching.

Ø

Outside, morning wakes my mother. Groggy on her back in the double bed, she wears torn boxer shorts. Tries to lift her head but feels like shit, lets it sink back again. Eyes flutter shut. One, two, three ... A woman down for the ten count. Or until someone calls her. Mommymommy. Ref in a dirty diaper, shaking the ropes of the ring. The crib. Calling her; calling me.

My mother staggers to her feet and slopes down the hall to my brother's room. She lowers the crib bar and half lifts, half pulls Nick out of the pungent nest of Lion King quilt, Buzz Lightyear pillow. My brother kicks his feet, feeling for the floor. Hits rug running. Bursts from half-hearted tug at diaper tab.

Back in her bedroom my mother resumes her supine position, but the deep tides of sleep elude her now. Nick's feet are audibly drumming in the living room, dining room, shooshing in the carpeted hall. He moves rapidly from room to room, looking for something. The kitchen door bangs open, cupboards thud. — Nick? calls my mother, nervous now. But the kitchen door barks again. Nick barks back.

— 'erbil?

An alarming series of sounds in the hallway. He's just outside the bedroom now. My mother sighs. Hears but doesn't look to see him peeking, one dark eye laughing in the gap between door and jamb.

Footfall. Bed sag.

Spring creak and bed bounce. Nick joins us in the tangled sheets, calls my name and bangs on my roof. My mother, in a surprise burst of speed, catches his fat fist mid-blow, explaining why we don't hit Mommy's tummy. I can't help but agree — hitting her knocks my pictures off square and sends plaster down from the ceiling. Hitting Mommy makes a mess on the rug.

My mother lets go of Nick's hand and immediately he lands another thudding blow. Inside my mother, the chandelier swings. Outside, my mother cracks. There are splinters of ice in her mouth — she's as cold this morning as last night she was hot. There's frost-fuzz along facial faults, over cheek and radiant from eye socket — this morning my mother suffers freezer burn. Her hand wraps hard and cold around Nick's warm wrist. But she *strains* to defrost. She swallows, gulps. She ingests all those cold words. Says: Man.... Turns away.

And I'm turning away too, spinning in a darkened apartment. Obviously there's been some kind of failure, so light the candles, flick on the flashlights — just remind me where they're kept. Already, on the edge of my vision I see glacial tongues at the ends of hallways. And as my mother swallows all those ice cubed curses, our insides grow colder and colder until Gerbil shivers in the dark, feeling frost creeping from toe to knee to thigh. Numb fingers and numb toes, frozen and waiting — waiting for time to pass, for lights to breathe back on, for paws to thaw. Certainly there's been some kind of a failure, but what? Whose?

Ø

There's a clock in this vast mansion of mine, in the Great Hall. I wake up on the flagstone floor with no idea of how I got here. In fetal position I lie, having no one to tuck me in, to draw a comforter to my chin; I come to with a shiver. Only the clock bends over me, not at all solicitous. I see right up its nose into its workings, this chronometer with an unrivalled mechanism for keeping the time. I see the great metal cup — double chambered and bivalve like a clam — that squeezes out every second. Over and over the cup rusts, flushes the flux, and rusts again. On the hour, I watch as hands align. Golden orbs spin. Pendulum swings. Clock strikes the hour for story time.

Story time. My mother and Nick hang out in the sunny living room with the striped chesterfield. My mother droops over throw cushions. Nick spins on the rug. He's overwound, wound up, uptight, tightly wound.

— Other children nap when they get tired, says my mother. But Nick ignores her, keeps spinning.

— Come sit beside me, Nick.

— Story! Nick scrambles onto the chesterfield, fortifies himself with throw cushions, sits with feet spread, fists up. Clearly my brother loves literature.

My mother sighs, reaches into the basket, selects a board book to read to Nick while Nick begins to bounce up and down on the chesterfield. Seems like forever that I've been in this robin's egg and sunshine room, hypnotized by the flip-book blur of my brother's rebounding face.

The board book holds twelve thick pages, aggressively white and empty except for spare illustration, elliptical comment. One of those books. A fat and happy toddler looks for, finds, oddly dispersed articles of clothing: yellow socks, green shoes, blue hat. To celebrate, he crawls off toward a purple balloon. My mother breaks off her reading, distracted by a brush stroke that curves around the nip and tuck of a pen and ink diaper. She sits quiet, just looking. Her eyes flit, skip, jump from line to flow of shadow shaped pigment — the most active she's been all day. A lash-lift above the diaper, there's a lovely curl of paint for the balloon — purple paint pools dark at rubbery mouth, stretches thin and dry over bulge. String dangles, finishing in a faint scumble of ink, just graspable. My mother puts her finger on the drawing. There's an itch in that finger.

Nick hears the silence and stops bouncing. He leans up against my mother, attempts to force himself behind her back. Possession is nine-tenths of the law. — Mommy, he claims.

— You weren't listening, Nick.

— BALLOON, insists Nick.

— Okay then, what colour was the balloon?

— Boy. Balloon.

— But what colour?

— Balloon, says Nick. Balloonballoonballoon.

My genius brother.

My mother sighs echoingly, hauntingly, draftily. Nick takes another board book from the pile. The winter sun slants sideways, and wet, mucky traffic noise rises from St. Clair outside. My mother heaves, hos, takes the new book from Nick. Nick now tries to come and sit on her lap, but I'm there, like a tire-jack in her gut. My mother groans, fends him off gently, protests too much. Nick climbs down, stands square on the ground in front of her, his hands dangling slightly.

I just know what he's thinking. — Finders keepers, I tell him, finding at last the correct legal precedent with which to contest his grubstake. That's the law. Finders keepers. Losers weepers.

Nick won't give me the satisfaction of showing me I've won. Dry-eyed, he turns away, wanders the length of the radiator, a little lawyer in diapers rehearsing the facts in the case, considering grounds for a new claim.

— Book, commands courtroom Nick, turning, lifting his hand from the radiator fin. He studies my mother, who is his judge and jury.

— Okay, Nick, says my mother, chucking Nick's book to the end of the chesterfield. Nick begins to protest, but she takes a new book off a side table — a paperback with a battered cover —

and opens to the first page. She begins to read to us; in a sing-song voice, she reads to us in the afternoon sunshine, and Nick falls silent. And as she reads, a boat forms from the hardwood of the living room floor, a ship with creaking masts and fluttering sails. Arctic seas lap at the throw rug. Icebergs form in the radiator's warmth. Down in the cabin, a story nestles in, a story like a baby in a womb; on the floes, a monster waits with a tale of its own.

Nick throws himself on the chesterfield beside her. Stands up tall on striped cushions, begins bouncing. At any time now, I think, waiting for the drop-roll, the bored scream, the casual detonation of afternoon stillness. But surprisingly Nick only bounces and seems to listen as my mother reads, way over his head. She stops once or twice and Nick stops too, bounces when she starts. She toys with him, but he's serious. — More, he says, missing her voice already.

Down in the hold, she booms like a breaker. I've slipped under hatches like the silvery fish I am. Unable to help myself, I slide down, down to the bottom of her where the only sound is muted and dull. Down to where metal pipes twist and turn overhead, leaking drop by drop. Puddles forming on the floor, dark without reflected light. A single light bulb dangling sends a dull, round, cheese-yellow swinging across the surface. Forked shadows lie left, then right, then left again. Salt water in a tin cup. Wet rope. Everything lost on a voyage at sea slides down and down, collects at helm crease, at hull fold. Rusted spanner. A pirate's earring. A candle stub, waxy as an ear.

I, Gerbil, stop and rest my pointed chin in my delicate paws. I sigh and pause and sigh again. Not much time has passed since the whale song, the lung liquid, the wet behind my ears, but I know I look older already — tiny circles under my huge, dark eyes, a hint of a frown line on my forehead. I'm giving nothing away — too canny for that, too much your consummate narrator. Still, perhaps things are more complicated than I'd guessed: more characters, more perspectives, more pairs of eyes, sets of lungs, tongues flapping. More rolling eyes. More slick cheeks. More dirty fingers.

I pricks up an ear; I shakes my head. Start again.

This story is a job site. This story is a slick operation. Her and me. The salt and the blood. The bubbles of breath. Knew I'd a task ahead of me, looked forward to hard work. Gerbil in a hard hat. Gerbil with steel toed boots. Gerbil with plumber's butt, her tool belt fully loaded. Cranking, hammering, twisting — unclogging the blocked pipes of our story.

And if complications should emerge from one of those pipes — Nick distending the copper like a python's breakfast — who would begrudge me a moment to catch my breath? Now, while Nick bounces, while my mother reads. Gerbil, curled up tight, chin to knees. Who would hold the need for a moment's peace against a hard-working rodent? Anyone? Then, hush.

MY MOTHER.

What a maroon. What a gullible. I'm coyly quoting here: the Epistle of St. Bugs. Remember how the Saint stands, hardly twitching his holy rabbit ears, while the cartoon bull runs back and forth, back and forth, snorting and steaming and pawing the ground? That bull is the very picture of my mother sleeping. Back and forth she rolls in eggshell sheets, breathing in bursts, not pawing but fingering the blanket's edge. My mother disturbed in sleep by dreams of babies. Not nightmares exactly. Something else in the half-light of the room, something lost in the untranslated sounds she makes. Facing left, and the outer wall, she mumbles. Rolling. Facing right, and the inner wall, she gibbers obscurely. Gibbers: the only word for the sound that she makes facing right. Gibbers. Mumbles. Rolls. And at the foot of the bed, my brother Nick, watching.

Oh, my brother, here we go again. I know what's on your mind: Nick murders Sleep. A crime of passion. Nick's the kind of guy to pop Sleep with a lucky punch; Sleep's teeth tinkle on the floor. Sleep sways, staggers. Sleep's out.

Nick's in.

Nick goes undercover. Lightning fast, he climbs beneath the blankets. My mother hardly wakes before my brother's skull connects — a punishing blow to her cheek that rattles my windows. She moans and contracts, covering her forehead with her hands, while Nick sees his main chance. He untangles himself from bedding and lies back upon the pillows. Morning light streams for a millisecond between his cocked feet and my mother's unprotected back. Then Nick fires his heels, double-barrelled — bang, bang — and my homegirl takes a direct hit. The motherland sits up in bed, vibrating with complaint. Like a shot, Nick falls on her, patting her down, searching for vital signs, vital sighs, any proof of motherly love. My mother shoves him off her. Laughing,

Nick approves the game and comes back for more. He likes the sensation of being lifted and pushed back against the pillows. He lunges again, falls backward, rolls hilariously, hits his head on the wall, and laughs all the harder. My mother's contribution is grimmer, not so much a game.

My mother puts an end to play, gets up, escapes into verticality. Nick knows himself disadvantaged when she stands. Even sitting on the bed he is only thigh-high, no place for a dude, and so he stays in bed, burrowing in sheets with an enthusiasm that I can only approve. My mother watches him, nursing injuries, hard to read. She turns on her heel, limps away.

Over by the dresser, we have a good look at ourself in the oval mirror. We notice how facial planes crumple, deep-sea trenches open under eye slits. Not a bad face once but aged beyond repair, fabulously decrepit — oh how she does go on. She even finds some wrinkles too. My poor old mother, I say out loud, thinking of my Polaroid, knowing I glow rosier now than on that first exposure. We're waxing and waning, she and I. A simple matter of the transformation of matter — old moon into new, her into me — confirmed by astronomy. But still, how sad to see your pitted lunar surfaces, my poor old mother. I rub my finger and thumb together — the world's tiniest violin. Hey, hey. Look whose finger; look whose thumb: the newest, most lovely digits in the world.

My tiny fingers. My tiny fingernails. My tiny lashes. The Gerbil fan club regrets my mother's swollen, fat fingers. Mine curve like teacup handles. My mother's gums bleed. I have flawless tooth buds in my pink pout. Whole marbled slabs of my mother jiggle as she makes her way to the toilet. I, by way of contrast, have almost no body fat. I am the youngest and the thinnest — no one is younger or thinner than I. I could, if I wanted, score an agency contract. Gerbil, Supermodel. Sound appealing? My otherworldly look could be the next big thing. Big head and stick limbs, haute couture hanging perfectly from my pointed shoulders. A natch for the catwalk. London? Paris? Why not? I can uncurl from this fetal position for seconds at a time. And everyone knows, the really big names all end up fetal anyway — I just have a head start. Flash. Cover girl Gerbil. Me, with my white lashes and sticky eyes newly opened like a kitten's (mewling — those bright lights hurt). I've got the cutest little baby face, a darling puss. I'll say it again, no one's younger or thinner than I am. But hurry, hurry. I'm getting older and fatter. Even now, even me. My time is now. Sure, I'm not exactly viable outside the womb, but I see no problem. I'll be an arthroscopic celebrity, an intrauterine star. A big shot on a really, really tiny sound stage.

Nick calls to my mother from the bed. She's still looking at herself, thinking, turning her head from side to side, watching herself in the mirror. Fingers on temples, she lifts her face, turns three-quarters, cheekbone right, eyes left. My mother sighs. Nick calls her from between the crumpled sheets. — Up, Mommy. Mommy? Up? She goes to fetch him, brings him back to the mirror, curious about the contrast between her skin and his (worse than expected). Now they both stare back from the mirror. Nick bounces baby blues off the mirror, geometric as billiards. My mother, our Madonna of the eye-ball-in-the-corner-pocket, touches her chin to his fluttering temple.

Ø

Outside the bathroom window, the soft drifts of snow have solidified to plugs of ice; the window sprouts ferns of frost, the mould of winter. Every night, the steam of bath time dissipates, slipping out through cracks in the grout, crusting on surfaces, scumming glass and tile. In the mornings, the yellow walls are paler, colder, dirtier, more depressing for my mother who sits on the hard side of the tub with her hands clasped on my roof. With the bathroom door between Nick and herself, my mother rests on cold porcelain and feels sorry for herself. She has a gift for self-pity, my mother — she really does. Listen. Whispered complaints twist her lips. My mother minges.

Minge — a word my mother uses with Nick. She says things like: *stop minging or I'll tear the veins out of your other arm.* Recognize the joke? The one about the boy who wouldn't eat his blue spaghetti? Not that my mother makes that joke out loud — not to Nick's face anyway — but she whispers. She thinks really, really loud. She makes faces. Grimaces. Smiles to herself. Up in my tower, with my telescope, I have her between the cross hairs. She might be in the kitchen. Nick might be dripping jam or spilling juice or kicking the rungs of his chair. She might be cringing at the mess or at the noise or pretending to be oblivious with her hands deep in dishwater. I see her mutter into corners, crack wisecracks for ... cracks. I see her mouthing things in pot lids, in metal bowls, in shiny tiles, in the convex backs of spoons. My terrible mother, with her pinhead, her giant nose, her tapering chin, her two fat lips uttering phrases that drip with the lard of self-pity, eaten whole. Or spread thick on slices of bread. My mother, licking her lips. Smiling through her tears, both consumed and nourished.

She thinks she's funny, but I've swum to the site of her funny bone and found nothing there, only an empty hollow suggestive of postpartum shrivelling. No glad-gland, Dr. Gerbil diagnoses. Sorry, Mom, but the damn thing just dried up. Ashes to ashes. Dust to dustpan.

My mother stops smiling, sighs again. Nick lurks outside the door of her wintry bathroom. Grasping the towel bar, she pulls us to her feet. My tower room tilts a little, rights itself. My telescope swings down, then up. I put out a hand and steady the swinging instrument. Already my mother is at the sink, splashing water on her face, avoiding the mirror in this cold, heartless light.

Ø

Today is the day for my mother to clean the house, a stab at normalcy and not a moment too soon. Dust lies thick on the radiator, untouched by human hands save where Nick delves, begriming cheek and nostril. Fingerprints festoon walls. Below these celebratory smudges, ominous coagulants of hair and lint collect in corners, forming committees, climbing on soapboxes, plotting, planning the revolution. Through all this my mother wades, oblivious to the unrest beneath the soles of her dirty feet. She heads for the broom cupboard, her mood both grim and fell. Dressed in old clothes, she twists up her hair with an elastic, warning Nick of her intentions.

I have my doubts. I may be under house arrest, but I'm far from idle. Like I said, I'm watching her. There are things I know that I didn't before. I know that the dusting defeats her. Vacuuming vanquishes her. The washing — that's the worst — the washing makes her weak. Now I know about the overflowing basket in the bedroom closet: her own holey underpants, those oddly large T-shirts, the damp sheets and mossy towels.

Nick's training pants.

I understand my brother a little now. We communicate not in words or glances but in DNA, the twisted helix of siblinghood. Nick wears training pants to train our mother to do the laundry. He frequently dirties those sad, grey flags of interdependence so that she can get as much practice as she needs. He and I agree the task is simple: strip Nick bare, rinse bum, dry bum, find new but clean sad and grey training pants, call Nick, call Nick, chase Nick, catch Nick, force Nick into clean pants, rinse dirty pants, roll washer across the room, attach washer to sink, detach washer from sink, do dishes, reattach washer to sink, wash pants, partially dry pants, blow fuse, find fuse in drawer, find that new fuse is not new, wrap new fuse in tinfoil, restart dryer, worry about power bill, worry about fire hazard, remove partially dry pants from dryer, hang pants from kitchen ceiling to dry completely, find pants with face in night when getting Nick a drink of water, pick up flung but still not dry pants from corner in morning, replace damp pants in Nick's drawer, replace damp pants on Nick, five minutes later strip Nick bare.... Is that so much to ask?

Still, our mother is stupid and slow to learn. The pile of training pants grows ever higher, making the apartment stink (although only when the radiators work). Sometimes all she does is stare, willing the mound to disappear. Wasting time. Procrastinating. Prevaricating. Sometimes she curses the pile, gently if Nick is present (You stupid laundry), descriptively if Nick is occupied elsewhere in the apartment (You heap of shit). Sometimes the black bile roars around my mansion walls, washing my window with her useless, pointless rage.

What makes her so angry? She hates the vacuum. She hates the mop. She'd hate the feather duster if she had one. She loathes the stove. She wants the stove to have an accident, to fall from the fire escape into the concrete alley below. My mother riffs on this fantasy whenever she cooks. She stirs a pot of spaghetti sauce, lifts the spoon, and while the sauce drips back into the pot, considers the smash. Fractured bones of porcelain and chrome. Hemorrhaging wires. Screws bouncing up the alley like broken teeth. The police would come; the neighbours would call them. My mother imagines herself in the shadow of her kitchen, strobe-lit by the ambulance's futile flashing. *That stove was depressed, Officer,* she'd tell him (tall, handsome in his uniform). *I don't think it was an accident.* He'd nod, make a note. Of the light on her sculpted cheekbone. On her raven's wing hair.

Ha.

∅

Today is the day for my mother to clean the house. She feels driven to this drastic action, compelled by some vague sense of something lost. My mother stands in front of the broom cupboard, her hair elasticated into a messy knot, her oldest sweatpants showing her grey knees. Nick comes up behind her and shouts so loud she shouts back. Then worries. Who might have heard her? What would they think? Someone could be dialing the bad parent bureau right now, informing on her in an angry voice. *Hello?*

Police? Come take away poor little Nicholas — his mother has been shouting again. But no siren sounds, no one hammers on the door: *Open up in the name of the law.* My mother is bad, all right, but not bad enough. Another failure to add to the grocery list. And soon Nick is audible down the hall, shouting at his stuffed mouse in his mother's voice. For her part, she lets go of the broom cupboard handle, puts her head in her hands.

Perhaps this isn't the day for my mother to clean the house.

Ø

Time passes by moon-wane, by sunrise. Time passes by the weight and length of me, by the timepiece in my splitting cells, in my fish bones, in my mutable tissues. Time passes by the ticking, teasing clock on my mother's kitchen wall. I know more of my mother than I did. And still time passes.

I've been watching her. I've been making a study of my mother while the blood clock pumps, while the heart clock beats. I know her insides from the inside. I know her face from the mirror, her crumpled smile, her crumpled frown. I know the grinding of her days.

My mother lifts her face from her hands, gives a cocktail yawn of fatigue, tedium, and stress. She closes her eyes and — in order to avoid the slumping of my tired walls, the sag of my exhausted ceiling — I close mine too.

Ø

My mother has found one of Nick's paintings behind the radiator in the bathroom. She can't imagine how it got there. Supporting herself with a hand on the wall she bends over the rising loaf of me and retrieves the dusty sheet of foolscap. I wish I could say that my brother's artistic efforts bring a smile to her face; I wish I could say she scoops the painting up gently and props it on the toilet tank in a place of honour. Instead, she pinches it between thumb and forefinger, lifting the picture for us to see. My mother stares at Nick's incoherent brushwork, at the paper's scored surface. Then, with a backward glance at an oblivious Nick, she lets the painting slip, lets it slide back behind the radiator.

Ø

The powdery, school marm pigments that my mother keeps in a cupboard in the hall, when added to water, produce super saturated paint like pigment gravy. But Nick's paintings — created in a frenzied eye-blink, preceded by twenty minutes of set-up and followed by twenty minutes of cleanup — are always the same colour. My mother gives him dandelion yellows, apple reds, sky blues. She pre-mixes popsicle pinks and glow-in-the-dark green. She experiments with the classic alizarin crimson or the technical cyan or the obscure periwinkle. But the colour of Nick's finished works never varies. Leaning over the sink and tipping excess paint down the drain, my mother tries to reproduce this exact hue. She mixes up the lemon of cleaning liquid, the cerulean of window wash, the emerald of dish soap. All the vivid shades of drudgery gurgle down my mother's drain. But only Nick can sour the sweetness of her candy-coloured paint. Only Nick can take a rainbow. And render it.

Conventional wisdom holds that mothers' kitchens are brightened by drawings of sunshine, happy houses, smiling stick families. Under the magnets of my mother's fridge hang carcasses, punching bags, wads of chewing gum. Nick sings after painting. He throws his brush from him, spatters the last few drops of paint. Then he perches on the living room radiator and crows. Behind him on the dining room table his latest work curls in at the edges, smokes, bursts into flame. Another burnt offering for my mother to tape to her cupboard doors. Grumbling, she hustles Nick from his Batman art apron, collects stained yogurt tubs, scrapes saturated brushes dry, sponges paint from table, floor, and wall. And pours the fouled, nauseous, sickening dregs of paint into the sink.

What is the colour of Nick's paintings? What is the colour of the land of my birth? Of the walls of my house? Puke Puce, Vomit Violet, Barf Beige? A nice Morning-sick Mushroom for the dining room? Up-chuck Umber in the den? The mind boggles. Eyes film, vision blurs. I see my mother in visual stereo: one channel has her hanging miserably over the sink, the other on her knees by the toilet bowl. Nick's paint brushes in the draining board, his painting behind the radiator — if only they weren't that colour.

Ø

Other things I've seen. Other things I've watched my mother do. I see Nick eat a hearty lunch and then explode. Chunks of macaroni and cheese blow across the kitchen table. My mother leaps to Nick's side, takes his temperature, wrings her hands. Man, she says to the skies.

Oh Man. She sounds even more vehement than ever. Luckily, her baby book lies close to hand with its Handy Chart of Childhood Illness in the back for easy reference. Opening the book, my mother becomes instantly sidetracked into Lyme disease, into meningitis, into Reye's syndrome, into anything really frightening. Eventually she finds Nick's symptoms listed under Tummy-Trubble — something like that, I don't remember what exactly — and reads what she already knows, what is already painfully obvious from the secondary puddle of lunch that Nick has just deposited weakly on the linoleum beside her chair.

My mother gently takes Nick to her room, to the big bed, and nestles him down under her quilt. He has shiny eyes and flushed cheeks. Nick smiles a tiny smile, says — Mommy stay, Mommy, p'ease? My mother kisses his forehead tenderly and lies down beside him.

Nick celebrates by covering the bedspread with the last of his macaroni.

Later, after she cleans Nick up and ensconces him instead on the chesterfield with the television on and a kitchen pot set close to hand, my mother reverts to type. She curses in the kitchen, ambles with the rolling gait of a street fighter toward the washing machine, gives it a shove. The wheels squeal. Tearing savagely at the hose, she jams it to the faucet with a deft upper cut. Then, snivelling bitterly, she attempts murder, forcing her vomit stained quilt deep into the machine's gaping mouth.

When did this happen? Maybe it was yesterday, maybe the day before that. I can't always tell. Time is a funny old fellow. My mother is less amusing. Still, she's a ticking timepiece all the same. A tick when she's happy, a tock when she's sad, the ringing of alarm bells when she's so damn angry. That's how we tell time around here.

Ø

Nap time. My mother tries to read whenever Nick sleeps. She now tries to read, something she's found lying near the chesterfield. She cracks the cover, and looks at the blurry, swimming print. What? What's it say? What's the matter with the focus? Whose book is this anyway? A book abandoned with a split spine. Something she tried to read while Nick was awake? She does that too, y'know, pretending to play with him on the floor, propping books open on chairs where she thinks Nick can't see. Or, when that doesn't work, she slips on her headphones, hiding them under her hair, trying to fool Nick with feigned attention to plastic farm animals. Down on her knees talking too loud. Nick stares, then reaches, pulls off the headphones. My mother says — What? What?!

Deprived of the above, my mother resorts to singing aloud. Well, how should I describe my mother's lullabies? Half-remembered choruses of punk songs, ancient radio epics, bits of club music from back when she was a grown-up allowed out after dark. But Nick climbs into her lap and puts his hand over her mouth. — P'ay.

— I'm paying, Nick, says my mother. — I'm paying.

Ø

Sometimes my mother reads magazines — really, she looks at pictures. Lifestyle magazines are her special weakness. Right now she's lying on her side on her bed. Nick naps next door. In front of her is a magazine, but look: glazed eyes, head bobbing like the float at the end of a fishing line. Her bedroom wavers. Goodbye to the battered bed, the blinds aslant, the T-shirts abandoned on bed and floor, that sock hanging from an open drawer. Hello to creamy walls, crisp linens, a mirror with a shining frame. My mother rises as if in a dream and wraps us in a luxurious bathrobe that neither of us have ever seen before. From somewhere appears a steaming bowl of café au lait. My mother sips, sitting on the window seat (new too — is that sawdust I smell?). The steam rises off her coffee; the little birds sing on the windowsill. Tweet tweet.

But, as in all dream sequences, the scene shifts (corny stuff, the visuals dissolve, form sine waves). Oh where are we now? The living room — I hardly recognize the place all bedecked and refurbished. I don't even know my own mother dressed in a pinstripe maternity suit (how ironically delicious — the *new* motherhood) or — do my eyes deceive me — does she sport a bolder look: belly-baring jeans and tie-dye halter. Whatever. Already, she sits at her little escritoire, calling a few friends on the telephone, laughing, chatting, inviting the dearest, the nearest, the bestest of them to dinner. Soon Joe from the butcher's down the street is ringing the bell, delivering the lamb for the entrée. My mother meets him at the door, teasing him in her serviceable Italian. His dark eyes appreciate her swelling beauty. He lingers in her doorway, flirts, but she taps him on the chest with her forefinger, asking after his wife, his mother. Nick emerges from his bedroom (yes, she needs him now), wanting her help with a very long word in a story he's reading. My mother bends down low to kiss Nick's cheek. Her skin against his is even smoother, even softer. Joe shakes his head admiringly. — *Si bella,* he says. *Si bella.*

Hang on. She's sending Joe away. Joe is too suggestive of a dirty joke. Joe is too much of an impolitic stereotype. Joe gilds the lily.

She focuses on Nick instead — Nick's a good direction for this fantasy. Nick can eat lunch with her at the Biedermeier table inherited from somebody's great-aunt. Nick and my mother will giggle their way through a basil pesto (her) and spaghetti (him) and she doesn't care if he drips tomato sauce. He turns his napkin orange — how they laugh.

More food. The gigot of lamb is in the oven in time for my mother to make Nick's supper (she insists on cooking for him herself although she needn't). She glows as she bends over the stove, fans herself, laughs as she prepares homemade cream of broccoli soup. Nick grins to see the crusty bread come steaming from the oven. — My favourite, he cries, enunciating clearly, perfectly. He loves his bread, his broccoli, and, after dinner, he loves his bath. My mother loves it too, so amused to see her boy in his beard of foam. Coyly, he splashes her and she splashes back, soapy water soaked up by the thick, white bath mat. Perched on the edge of a wingback chair, slip-covered in terry towel, my mother laughs and laughs. And laughs. And laughs.

Ding ding. Doorbell. Folding Nick into a super luxurious bath towel, my mother takes him with her, opening the door with a welcoming smile. Her guests chuckle and exclaim how charming to find Nick alfresco and my mother with bath bubbles clinging to the tip of her nose. — What a good mother, the guests whisper, as she bears Nick off to bed. What a very good mother.

Ø

Too much. Much, much too much. We both have to pay when my mother indulges like that. And so, when the real Nick wakes with an incoherent roar, my mother snaps back feeling worse than ever. See her eyes come up pupils, not cherries like a slot machine. A sour taste in her mouth. She gets up stiffly, stumps down the hallway, releases Nick from bondage, from cribbage.

You'd think he'd be glad to see her but he storms and rages at his mother, at the world, at the stuffed creature he takes to bed.

While my brother rails, beating crib legs, my mother's legs, with Mousie, his threadbare fetish object, I make my way into my own kitchen. I'm not feeling too great either, and, for once, my kitchen hardly helps. At my touch, the overhead light burns out in a shower of sparks. Illumination leftovers spill through red checkered curtains. Liver-coloured floor tiles cant. Walls throb, shudder, heave. Toss poor Gerbil to the refrigerator, looming palely in the gloom, a tombstone with a silver handle, a rubber seal. My paw, as I reach for the door, shakes, scrabbles on the smooth and stainless steel. Pull, Gerbil. Pull hard. Yellow light pours from inside, cream from the cool. I open my pink mouth. I drink. Something vaporous slides down my throat. Tendrils of steam lick my forehead, my upturned chin. My brow is rimed with frost. I shut my eyes and inhale. Levitating. Floating a foot from the ground.

My mother, in her kitchen, finds no such relief. She's muddle-headed, exhausted, can't think of why she came into the kitchen. — Why am I here, she asks of her reflection in the window. My mother's fevered interior lies shadowed from me as I float here in the cool breeze. My mother's intentions amount to a guessing game for a Gerbil. Twenty questions. Animal? Mineral? Pharmaceutical? No, no, no. Bottle of scotch? Nah. Crusty syringe? The thought makes me snort and snicker behind my paw. Gun or knife? Just enough rope? Ha. Whip, dildo, pair of split-crotched panties? Not very likely.

— What am I looking for? she says aloud.

She is not thinking straight, my mother. She never does. She blames hormones, making her fuzzy-brained, but hormones aren't the problem. Right now there are women in power suits making decisions, selling, buying. Surgeons bypassing hearts. Even as my mother blows her sorry nose, there are women ministers, saving the party, saving a soul. Women above us in the skies, hunched over glowing dials, fuel gauges. Women with wings breaking the speed of sound. There are women in space. Space women, colonizing Mars, bypassing Venus.

—Think, my mother tells herself. —Think, think.

Think, says I. Says Gerbil. How came you to be hostage to a cabal of plush toys, imprisoned in a fortification of cushions and blankets, ransomed to a piggy-banker for monopoly money? Think.

But my mother refuses. She evades all twenty of my questions. All twenty thousand. All twenty billion. My mother has found what she was looking for: only another magazine under a stack of flyers—on parenting this time. Same fat roll of glossy pages. Same spit-fingered rifling. Same centrefold: a lifestyle spread, all arched spine and playroom shots. Curvaceous toys from big city boutiques. European design strollers. Pots of luscious zinc ointment. Pouting nursing bras with frilly straps. An orgy of cookies.

Over the page, popovers steam on the back of a careful stovetop. Or pizza faces. Or oatmeal cookies. Muffins wear perfect pats of butter on their whole wheat heads. Melon balls, cubes of watermelon, slices of pears lie on a plate. A tub of carrot sticks awaits, pre-sliced on Monday for all week consumption. Treats playfully crouch behind cupboard doors—crackers, strips of fruit leather, cheese strings—a jack-in-the-box surprise for snack time. Healthy, and convenient in a pinch, because even good mothers are busy mothers.

My mother, neither good nor busy, turns pages, groans.

Ø

My mother finds what she's after, a special après-nap snack for Nick. She finds the recipe, studies the picture, reads the headline—Healthy Snacks Kids Will Really Eat. So she cuts up celery, spreads peanut butter, slices cheese and places on Nick's plate a decorated, smiling celery stick nestling on a bed of sliced cheese. Peanut butter fills the celery's long hollow causing it to beam up from the plate with contented raisin eyes. My mother sets the plate down before Nick with a special beam in her own eyes, bends over and kisses his dark head.

Nick goggles at the snack. The very second he begins to look doubtful, my mother sits herself beside him, scoops up a celery piece and begins to talk in a funny voice. — Hello, Nicholas, my name's Mr. Crunchy. Please eat me up.

Nick looks at my mother, darkly. He looks at his plate.

— Oooo, Mr. Nick has hurt Mr. Crunchy's feelings. Mr. Crunchy is so yummy. Mmmm.

— No, Mommy. Nick's voice is quiet and clear. Unusual for my brother, but then he clearly knows his own mind on the subject of Mr. Crunchy.

— Eat me up, Mr. Nicky. Look, Mommy loves me. Would you like to eat me, Mommy? Oh yes I would, Mr. Crunchy, but I'm saving you for Mr. Nick. Take a bite, Nick. Take a bite out of Mr. Crunchy.

My mother begins to walk Mr. Crunchy off his plate and toward Nick. Nick watches Mr. Crunchy come, scowls, and then tucks his own hands into his armpits. Mr. Crunchy presses onward, leaps from the plate, flies like a superhero. Nick flushes red, but bravely our celery hero heads directly for Nick's tightly compressed lips.

My mother experiences both pain and a surge of adrenaline resulting from Nick's swipe at the celery (and so, in a delayed fashion, do I). Already Mr. Crunchy is spiralling into the air, somersaulting upward and hitting hard against the window. He sticks for a second as if clinging to life, then slides, leaving a smear of peanut butter on the glass like ... well, I hardly like to say.

— Bad, cries my mother as she lurches from her chair, holding her forearm. — Oh Nick.

— No, Mommy.

My mother rushes to Mr. Crunchy's aid. She lifts him from the window ledge where he's fallen — noble soul — and looks down at the celery lying besmirched in her hand. Here, on the inside of my mother, I can hear the effort she makes: engine racing, gearsgrinding, brakes squealing. I smell the burning rubber. A loud dinging announces the arrival of a message from her brain. Incoming, incoming. Her mouth creaks — a drawbridge opened by minions but only under protest. Squeaking in an unnatural voice, my mother addresses her son. — So, you don't like celery, she says, patching a thin crust of good humour over the abyss of exhausted anger. — Well, we still have some cheese....

My mother falls silent as Nick picks up, one by one, the remaining slices of cheese on his plate. The cheese, flung with all his strength, misses the window and lands on the floor with a flat slap. Nick looks up at his mother. My mother. She turns to face the wall. — Ten. — Nine. — Eight.

But in the microwave's dark face I can still see Nick, reflected like his own evil twin. I see him reach out and, with a pudgy fist, smack the edge of his plate. Raisins erupt. The plate follows. Rotates mid-air. Falls. Spins, then clatters to a stop at my mother's feet.

A long silence.

Finally, my mother squats, picks up the plate. She holds it as though she could snap it with her bare hands, but hurls it instead. The plate lands in the sink with a crash.

— *Fuck* Mr. Crunchy, cries my mother.

Nick screams with pleasure.

Ø

At last, this day, like the others, winds down, dwindles to a point. Wiped away, this day, like a runnel of snot by a brisk Kleenex. And — having been so long endured — the day now turns tail. Leaves dusk behind and dusk stays to dinner. Dusk loiters outside the kitchen window watching Nick struggle with his spoon. Nick looks out, sees tomato smears in the west. Looks over at my mother, who chews grimly, nodding yes. She too sees the strands of cloud, stretched and pasta pale. A food throwing motif haunts them this evening. Contrite, they both hope for a better tomorrow. Their dark heads bend over their plates as they study the entrails of their dinner. Will a new day dawn or will morning porridge hang heavy in the sky? Sunny side up or sunny side down?

I'm no oracle. I know only this: my mother begins to droop over dinner dishes, leaves the pasta pot in the sink to soak. She washes, dries a few spoons, then stands drearily with the dishcloth in her hands. Applies a clean fingertip to the wall switch, flooding kitchen tiles with dirty yellow street light. My mother wrestles Nick into bed, where he falls asleep at last, exhausted by his long battle to stay awake. From my privileged position, I predict she won't manage to stay up long enough to watch the news, and I win the bet. My mother climbs into bed, crumpling into sleep over her magazine. Folded pages crease her cheek. The bedside light shines on and on. Outside, the night isn't a chocolate cake sprinkled with sugar stars, while fat flakes of mashed potatoes fall.

My mother wakes, rubs her cheek, switches off the bedside light. Thinks of her day. Thinks, it's over. Thinks, has it started yet?

Ø

But like so many others, this day has a coda, a stumbling-to-her-feet ovation. Back by popular demand. Crying. Vomiting. Hours of sleepless worry. Tonight, a noise wakes us in what feels like the middle of the night — a bowel-loosening, bone-shaking, eyeball-buzzing noise. My mother sits up, glances wildly left and right. The windowpanes are dark; they rattle in their frames. She hears Nick's voice, almost inaudible, crying fretfully from his crib. Calling her. Without so much as a thought for me and my comfort, my mother rushes to my brother. I jiggle and jerk down the hall. My four-poster is a waterbed now, lurching and undulating. I straddle the fluid mattress, ride the motion all the way to Nick's room. That's me, one arm in the air, cowboy style.

My mother scoops up Nick and holds him close to her, rocking from side to side. She soothes him while frowning hard through the damp strands of hair in her face. An unhappy sweat. An angry woman. — It's the middle of the night, whispers my mother. That's the sort of speech she usually reserves for Nick, but tonight the presence of music in her apartment gets the benefit of her ray gun disapproval. She hugs her son closer in what I imagine she imagines to be solidarity. Nick squirms. — Listen to that noise, she says to Nick, in a voice that makes him sit still. Nick looks up at her uncertainly. — It's *late,* my mother says. — Really, really *late*. Firmly, she speaks. She presses the light on her wristwatch. The display reads 9:40 PM.

I say, Come on, Mom. Listen. Don't be such a pain, Mom. What's the matter with you? Why are you so mean? Noise, you say? Well Gerbil hears a joyful sound. A dancing pulse. Come on, listen to the familiar beat — an aortic slam, a surge, an ardent tattoo. Blood comes home through the heart's front door. The music breathes — a long exhalation, like a newborn shout in an empty room. In a rib crib. In a pelvic apartment. Body music. Breathing and pumping music. Music for arms and legs. For fingers and toes.

A Gerbil dancing is a smooth and graceful thing, especially so in my case. My dance hall is liquid, and so are my movements. In truth, I dance naturally, better than anyone you ever saw. The beat animates me. I sway. I twitch. I dance on my little feet and know my prancing is divine. My mother feels me dancing, can only shake her head. The set of her chin, the scowl on her face, makes dancing harder. And worst of all, she makes plain the thing I lack: not polish, not comeliness, not refinement, but someone with whom to dance.

I say, Get up and dance with me, mother. I'm inviting you. Just this once. True, you have no native grace. The wave of your hand, the tilt of your head, the swing of your hips: you make these movements tightly, stingily. But maybe you could learn —

rehabilitation just might be possible. And I'm offering, just this once. Come on Mom, get up and dance with me. Or if you won't dance, at least let Nick up from under your arm. Let him dance with Gerbil.

But my mother never listens. —Too much noise, she repeats, working herself up to action. Clutching Nick to her she stomps toward the hallway door. Unwillingly, I must precede her, still dancing. My mother takes one step, two steps, three.

But even as she seizes the knob, the music stops. Has she squeezed the song into silence? Have her strong fingers on the brass extinguished the beat? In silence, my mother twists the deadbolt, flings open the door. Out on the landing, the door that mirrors our own stands closed and mute. No footfalls, bumps, scrapes sound from the bright rooms across from us. The lights aren't on, and nobody's home. No one at all. Just my jelly-bellied mother. Just my gut-wrenched mother. Just my bum-tummied mother. Just a foolish girl.

Ø

The night continues. Her sleep continues, interrupted by inaudible rhythms that come from rooms that I furnish, that I light. Whispers and soft laughter issue from behind walls she calls by other names, plasterboard she kneads under fingertips. The susurrating sounds of possibility keep her awake. But her sleeplessness extends on and on into the night. Nick breathes evenly and deeply, lying beside her in the big bed. But my mother mutters into the dark, begrudging everything she cannot quite hear. She resents the drinks, the lights, the party in her mind keeping her awake. She tries to count sheep (three in living room, deep in conversation), to count olives (two per martini), to count kisses (one on both cheeks). She enumerates everything she sees: the shining rows of plates and glasses, the coats heaped on the hostess' bed, the circle of faces in candlelight. Good times are narrow-cast on her bedroom's nighttime walls, roll like a private screening on the ceiling, on the insides of her lids. She makes me smile, shake my head. Doesn't she know? Doesn't she realize? The plates are mine, as are the glasses. I am the hostess. It is my face she sees in candlelight. Gerbil, in a top hat, dancing on the ceiling still asking, Will you? Won't you? Won't you dance with me?

And when at last she sleeps, she tosses and turns, rolls back and forth. Gibbers. Dreams of babies saluting like Boy Scouts, dreams of St. Bugs, of a wisecracking rabbit. Dreams of an absolution in consonants and vowels. Dreams of an 'I.'

I, on the other hand, dream of nothing.

I HAVE A FATHER.

Why didn't my mother tell me? Now why didn't I guess? He's only just arrived with a suitcase and guitar, standing in the hallway with his key in hand. My mother calls him Mahon but Nick calls him: Daddydaddydaddy.

— Nick. Hey, man. Hey li'l guy.

Nick runs to the kneeling Mahon, chest to chest, like smashing atoms. Mahon is knocked back on his heels, steadies himself with one arm, pulls Nick closer with the other. — Missed you, he says, mumbling, stubble in black boyhair. I take stock: the man in the hall has thick black hair, blue eyes. A sad smile for my mother, a loving bruise of a father.

My mother presses that bruise, gets both pleasure and pain. — What are you doing here? she demands, as if this weren't Mahon's own front hall, as if she weren't Mahon's own wife. In answer, Mahon rises, comes over to her, leans into her, tries to inhale her all at once. My mother lets him lean, but won't put her arms around him; she won't. — Two months' work, you said. It's still only six weeks.

— Maeve, says Mahon, groaning. He puts his arms around her but she stands rigidly. Nick comes over to crouch in the tent of their legs. He squats and grins, one hand on my mother's leg, one on Mahon's. My mother shifts her leg, meanly. Patiently, Nick repositions his hand.

— What happened to Parry Sound?

— The agency called, killed the booking.

— Yeah, well there's other places to play.

— We re-booked. Collingwood. But the van croaked in Barrie. It's totally fucked.

— Mahon.

— I mean, it's broken down. It's in a service centre in Barrie.

Mahon lifts his head from my mother's hair. Closer up he's

chapter three

older, his eyes are shot with red. He takes a step away from my mother and rubs his mouth with the back of his hand, looking at his suitcase, his guitar.

— Where's the rest of it? says my mother, waving her hand. — That's just the Gretsch.

Mahon shakes his head again, like he doesn't want to talk about his gear. But my mother does; she pushes the point. The amp? The pedal boxes? The Fender?

Mahon takes off his coat and carries his suitcase down to the bedroom. The gear is in the van, he tells her at last, unzipping the suitcase he's set on the bed. In the van that's in a service centre in Barrie.

— In the *van*?

— 's okay. Van's locked; Dave's there.

— But?...

— Maybe they think we can't pay for the work.

— But they have the van.

Mahon snorts. — Worth four-fifths of f— . He catches himself this time, looks down at Nick. — Of nothing.

— I don't get it.

Mahon looks up from rummaging in the suitcase, stares out the window. He doesn't look at my mother while he tells her how he came home on the Greyhound, through the night, through the snow. He came home to see her; he couldn't stand missing her, missing Nick.

— Mahon, says my mother, the stranger called Maeve. — Oh Mahon.

I say nothing. I'm not ready to say anything at all.

— Here it is, says Mahon, reaching into his suitcase. He holds out two fists, there's something hidden in one. He tells Nick to guess which. Nick guesses the left.

— Guess again, Mahon tells him.

Nick guesses the left. Again.

— One more time, Nick, says Mahon, rolling his eyes, laughing in my mother's direction. Nick considers, then once more taps Mahon's left hand.

— Nick, says my mother. Not hard to guess what she thinks of this display of my brother's maladroit thinking: dyslexia, ADD, lead poisoning. Baby books can be horror stories.

Mahon turns over his hands, opens them. There's a matchbox tow truck parked on his left palm. The joke's on my mother.

Mahon laughs and laughs. —The look on your face, says Mahon.

∅

We all end up in the living room. This is later in the day — much later. Time scheme grows a little fuzzy, but hey, you want absolute coverage, get yourself a video camera. Mahon vacantly strums his guitar, a different guitar this time, a big honey-toned Martin that came out from under the bed. See what I mean? How did I miss it? Was it there the whole time? And how did I miss his shoes in the hall, his hat on the hook, his shirt hanging from a drawer filled with his socks? There were telephone calls; they talk about conversations I never heard — how did I miss them? I was there; I *must* have been there.

And my mother, her endless sighing. Not, *man* ... that's not what she said. Not what she says as she watches him from the cane chair. Across the room, Nick drives his new tow truck up and down his father's socked foot. Nick knew. Even Nick.

I'm ready to say something now. I have a few questions I need to ask, like, who the hell does this woman, this Maeve, think she is? I'm the double agent; I'm the mole in this story, the Gerbil underground. She's a liar; she's tricky, not dependable. What kind of a mother is she? Keeping mum while all the time she had this stuff, this powdered adoration stored away, deep inside, a bag of heroin in a false-bottomed suitcase. And now she's sitting there, gazing at him, slack-jawed. Disgusting. Nauseating.

Mahon plays, picks with fingers, frets with a glass slide. The music whines and whinges and so does my mother, running through a theme and variations for the man on the chesterfield: the sometimes-here-sometimes-gone Mahon of her dreams.

Look. Do you see it? A picture on the mantel I never saw before. I see it now: Mahon playing straight-armed, head down, giving the backward grin, the look for the boys that says, *and a-one and a-two and a-one, two, three.*

My mother riffs on, sings Mahon the blues of her life: the laundry blues, the mealtime blues, the sleeping-alone-with-a kid-in-my-bed blues. And while my mother moans, my father nods, doodles on his guitar, twists his lips into sympathetic smiles at all the right moments until my mother's round, fat whole notes turn to rests, and my father drops bright, fast tones into the spaces she leaves behind. Soon, Mahon begins to strum and sing nonsense songs to make Nick laugh. He plunks on the strings and sings: *Nicknicknicknick.* Then, ear down to the bridge, he picks out a delicate harmonic, sings: Mae-e-e-e-*ve,* Mae-e-e-e-*ve.* He watches her with one eyebrow lifted, makes my mother smile — a real smile this time, from the inside to the outside. Everything in my room curves up — window frames, door frames, picture frames. Everything around me grins.

But my father is moving now, coming closer to where we sit in the wicker chair. What's he doing? I see him make himself comfortable on a side table directly beside us. Mahon sits knee to knee with my mother and the big Martin hangs only inches away from her belly. Now Mahon begins to play. He's right beside me; he's just on the other side of the wall. And I hear. I *hear* him play. Not through my mother's ears, not second hand like everything I've had 'til now. But with my own ears. Me. Gerbil. Mahon plays for me. With his guitar, he bridges the gap between present and future. He takes a bit of time, brushes off the shadows, the echoes, the reverberations, and gives it to me, bright and shiny. As new as on the day I will be born.

Mahon plays. He stops. He puts his lips to my mother's belly and kisses her. Kisses *me.* Softly calls: Hello? Hello, hello?

— 'erbil in dere, Nick tells him.

— Gerbil? says Mahon, smiling. Mahon looks at my mother, laughs to see her blushing. — Gerbil, says Mahon, trying it out.

And I call him in return. In my littlest voice. All I have left.

Daddy.

Ø

I think I'll be a runner when I get out of this fix I'm in. I like the idea of foot to pavement, setting down my sole on something hard. There's nothing hard in here. Nothing difficult. Just spongy walls and a certain lack of light. No challenges beyond my soggy mother with all her sad ways, and what kind of a challenge is she? Punch her and she jiggles; kick her and she slops back, an unset dessert. I could spin egg beater legs endlessly in the sloppy twilight of her and never make meringue. No, I'd like to get someplace, to run far in the sunlight. In any weather at all. I'd like to run in rain and snow, get wet, get cold. I'd like to be out of breath. I'd like to breathe at all.

Why is it that whenever people want to praise a safe, comfortable place they call it womblike, as if the womb were as good as it gets? Well, I have news for people. As accommodation, in utero bites big. And speaking of biting, think of the room service available in Hotel Womb. Yolk. Amniotic fluid scrambled with a little salt. What kind of food is that? A meal to be avoided, that's what. Leftovers up a fleshy straw — always the same damn flavour. Placenta. And the after-burn of afterbirth.

Pre-digested. Pre-papped. Pre-païd. Room and bored.

My father is a runner. Daddy gets up early in the morning. He sits on the side of the bed, tying laces while my mother watches him from amongst the crumpled sheets. My mother blinks, her brain stuck at a primeval level, preoccupied with inarticulate body function. She grunts, rolls on her side, scratches her belly, rolls back. Back-lying ranks as a risk-taking activity, baby book-prohibited for the pressure put on internal organs. My mother has already taught herself to scrupulously avoid sleeping belly up, arms and legs spread, head back, snoring like a lord — even in sleep she guards against herself. But now, with Mahon tying his laces on the bed beside her, my mother cuts loose. She lies on her back and gives evidence of enjoying the support up and down her spine. Her breasts dribble down her rib cage, forming a puddle under each arm. Her belly flattens as my room loses height and gains width. The ceiling comes into view, both hers and mine, and my mother smiles. Recollects. Smiles again.

I know what I'm supposed to do at this point in the story, what anyone — what everyone — expects of a Gerbil in my position. The time has come for kissing and telling, for telling about kissing. Everyone knows readers read ahead, parsing for dirty words, for smut even in texts as pristine as Gerbil's. Moans and groans. Fingers and tongues. Readers let the book fall open, hoping to happen on thrustings and suckings and strokings — the inside, inside story.

Come *on*.

I won't pander to extra-natal voyeurism. I won't produce pornography for the gyno-curious. Nor will I cater to those of you with special tastes, with literary appetites for innuendo, for sexual metaphor. I won't pimp to word lust, to lexo-lechery. I won't; I'm better than that. I'm a pure Gerbil — and don't even *think* the word 'prude.'

Besides, I was asleep. I missed the whole thing.

My mother obviously didn't. She sighs contentedly, leaving me — leaving us all to draw our own conclusions. Her eyes roll toward Mahon who, being a runner, laces up his shoes, pulls on a T-shirt, a sweatshirt, a watch cap for his head. — Maeve, he says, turning to her. He looks so cool in his track pants. My mother smiles again. Grunts. Rolls back up onto her side. Her exercise over for the day, she kisses my father before he turns and heads out for his. — Um-m-m, says my mother and licks her lips. A woman-puddle in the middle of the bed. Watch her lie back, listen to the runner's tread in the hall, the squeak of the deadbolt, the gentle thud of the door.

Another squeak. Another thud. Bare feet in the hallway and Nick appears in the door, crying Daddydaddydaddy. My mother sits up as quickly as she can, hands over belly, then out to catch Nick as he comes flying, leaping, diving through the air.

Son of a runner.

∅

Together my mother and Nick pull up the blind and sit on the radiator where they can see Mahon as he emerges from their building for his run. The day is crisp, the sidewalks clear. A little cold is good for a runner, and Mahon finishes stretching against the brick of their apartment, just out of sight. Now, he begins his slow lope along the sidewalk. Warming up. Breath visible in the cool air. Nick puts his head against the window and pushes, straining to see until my mother pulls him back, cautions him against cracking the glass. Nick slaps at her restraining hand. My mother grabs his wrist and pulls his fingers to her mouth, sucks them, kisses them. — No, says Nick, and he pulls his hand from hers, puts a finger into his own mouth. He stares intently out the window as Daddy gets smaller and smaller, his watch cap bobbing like a dot, dot, dot. All the way into invisible.

My mother sighs, tests Nick's diaper, squeezes with her finger and thumb. Nick twists, pulls his diaper from our mother's clutch. Now Nick bends his knees, throws out his arms and, with a shout, leaps from the radiator. He hits the ground running, burns carpet past the bed and into the hall. His feet sound all the way to the living room. In a moment, I catch the compressed sob of our depressed chesterfield followed by the silence-and-thud of the successful dismount. More footfalls run a rug's length, and then the drumming begins once again, a rat-a-tat-tat on the bare boards of his bedroom floor. Suddenly all noise stops. My mother and I wait on the radiator, the heat becoming intense through her thin nightshirt. She shifts a little. Then Nick reappears in the doorway, naked now. He pauses, strikes a pose, belly out, arms akimbo.

Nick. What a dude.

My mother follows him. We chase him down the narrow hallway and into the dining room. Nick runs, 'round the table and stops, laughing. My mother stops too, gestures, swallows a shout. She calls him once, twice, then she counts. One ... two ... three. Magic, as Nick disappears into the living room. There he dances, bum wiggling, elbows side to side, head back and forth until his face blurs, and all my mother can see is the grin, everlasting like the Cheshire Cat's. Finally my mother laughs too. She can't help herself. Victory makes Nick dance faster, wiggling downward onto the floor to roll like a man on fire.

— Careful, says my mother. — Careful, careful. The radiator fins are axe heads, the wooden floor full of jackknife splinters. Nick rolls to the chesterfield, wedges himself against the base, lies still, his face hidden under the dust ruffle. His skinny chest rises and falls, bird bones under the thinnest of covers. Nick's torso is matte and pale, enormous compared to his stick man arms and legs. He looks malnourished. My mother thinks of the times she's taken this kid to the swimming pool — holding the hand of Biafran Nick in his swimming trunks. — I do feed him, she says out loud. A joke, but no one laughs. Certainly not me.

Careful. What's he doing now? Skinny Nick lies still, but naughty Nick drums his feet. Xylophone ribs. The lady downstairs will complain. My mother takes a hit of anxiety and irritation: the goofball of motherhood. Now the fear valve opens, commences pumping, and she catches a double dose. There's dust under that chesterfield. Lead dust, mouse poop, other dangers unknown. My mother moves quickly, lurching forward on her own stick legs, more like her son than she'll admit. I catch her reflection in the blank TV screen, a wide, white shadow. Then she descends on Nick, rolling him over with a not-so-gentle hand. Nick smiles up at her. He's found something under the chesterfield. He's eating.

Ø

When my Daddy gets home from running, he's happy and relaxed. The red-faced grin he gives us from the doorway tells the whole story. He wipes his brow with a virtuous air. Good, honest, exercise. Early. Outside. Done.

My mother, on the other hand, has a face that's slick and shiny with tears. Nick lurks, red-eyed as well. Voices have been raised between the apartment's four walls. Tears have been cried. A much regretted smack has been loosed — vibrations still blur the room's edges. My mother regrets — but can do nothing about — the fact that Nick slips under her skin. He yanks her chain; she sputters, trying to explain. To Mahon. To herself. The things she says ... Starving and mouse poop but eating as well: her words make no sense. She makes no sense. Mahon's face falls. He takes off his watch cap. He rubs his head. Now his face tells another story.

Ø

We go grocery shopping. All of us need to get out of the apartment but none of us want to be here, trapped between yellowish tube lighting and greenish linoleum. Rows of shelving, hard honeycombs of box, can, and jar, stretch over our heads. Golden packages, golden cartons, golden pots, stacked but ready to come tumbling down at the slightest touch. Nick. My mother, standing mid-aisle, rubs her temples, considers the less-than-golden decisions that press harder every time she shops. Alchemy in reverse: the beginning of a leaden headache.

Shopping. Mahon holds the list, drives the grocery cart. Nick rides shotgun in the cart's metal baby basket. My brother has outgrown the fold-down seats and the narrow leg holes. His snow pants bulge, exposing the legs of his overalls. His shoes dangle below a foolish length of sock. He grins, a junior Don Quixote in flood pants, feet swinging like the country fair. Swaying, my brother prattles, editorializes, insults other shoppers. — Dats a very fat man, he tells my father who, cast against his will as faithful Sancho Panza, speaks for the first time since we entered these golden aisles.

— Shut up, Nick, he says.

— Well, says my mother. Uncomfortable. Suddenly businesslike.

I rub sleep from my eyes, having napped on the way here. Trying to disassociate myself for three long blocks: two down, one across. Drowsy despite the rise and fall of the maternal whine. A quiet Saturday afternoon if only she'd let me. The moment the apartment door closed behind us my mother began a gloss on the grocery budget. A fiscal screed delivered while pushing Nick's stroller through the slush. I tuned her out. Now, I'm not so sure I didn't miss something. A cold wind hovers over my nuclear family despite the unbuttoned coats, the unwrapped scarves. Someone sighs, or is it only the whisper of the automatic doors behind us? The grocery store, quiet as Tombstone before the gunplay. A cart wheel creaks. A fluorescent light flickers. From the acoustically-tiled heavens comes the inevitable announcement: Cleanup Required in Aisle Three. Not us. Not yet.

We shop. We leave the towering threat of the shelves and wander amidst the frozen food — there, where the glass doors reflect lost souls against banks of pizza, stacks of microwave macaroni. Arctic blasts from the plastic sacks of peas and corn cool us, sap us of our collective will. By the concentrated juice our hearts grow cold. My father opens a freezer door, reaches in, counts out frosty canisters of orange pulp. Three in total. He puts them in the cart. Adds one of lemonade. Quietly, patiently, my mother removes this last and goes to replace it in the freezer. Mahon, my father, watches her with narrowed eyes. The can escapes my mother's chilled fingers and falls to the floor, bouncing, rolling. She lumbers after it. I see my father eye her backside, notice the discolouration on one fleece-clad calf — dried tomato sauce, matted and red like a birthmark, and about as familiar. How long has it been there? Long time, for sure. Mahon's eyes narrow further, so icicle thin nothing gets past them. Beside him, Nick swings his feet and sings.

My father pushes the cart to the next freezer chest, opens the glass door and drops a frozen Key Lime Pie into the cart. For my part, I see no reason to assume that my father acts in a deliberately provocative way. His need for Key Lime Pie may be genuine, supported by a doctor's note. A legitimate budgetary expenditure.

My mother stands beside the cart, wringing her hands a little. Without another word, my father picks up the pie and cavalierly tosses it back on the shelf.

Whatever.

We file past the ice cream, the frozen desserts, the sherbet in rainbow colours. Nick looks longingly at the freezer door, at the abandoned box with its pert oval of citrus green. —Mama? he says tentatively before catching a blast of a cold front colder than anything the freezer can produce.

We trudge up and down aisles. Winter comes with us. We bring it, like that witch in one of Nick's books.

∅

Going home, real winter bites back. Pellets of snow fly like pebbles from an infant fist. The stroller bends and buckles under the weight of all the bulging plastic sacks hanging off handles. Nick walks beside my mother, his seat in the stroller taken by a bag of potatoes, a net purse of onions. Imagine. Nick sniffs, minges. He sees in his place a vegetative sibling: pumpkin head, radish nose, lettuce cap shoved down tight over mushroom ears. The child pumps his plump plum fists and kicks his zucchini legs, jeering at Nick from what rightfully belongs to Nick. My brother catches wind of his future and decides to sit down in the street, in the falling snow. His parents stare at him. They don't. Need. This.

My father can think of a hundred ways he'd rather spend a Saturday, and he tells my mother so. This makes her mad; I feel her heart begin to pound, her blood start to rush; but suddenly she can do nothing more than agree with him. Out here the cold is real. Her feet are numb. The plastic handles of the bags she carries cut into her mitten-clad hands. The laden backpack Mahon wears pulls him off-centre a degree or two, a tree in the winter wind. She smiles a little at that.

— Okay, Nick, says my mother, to her now roaring son. Best voice: tarts and gingerbread voice, bluebirds swooping voice.

— Come on, Nick, says my father, following her example. — Time to help out. Only two blocks.

— Up you get, Nick, says my mother. — Would you like a cookie when we get home?

Nick sits in the snow, wails even louder then flops onto his back, a starfish in a snowsuit. His face looks surprisingly red against the white snow. My mother bites her lip.

— I should have given him a snack before we came.

— He had a good lunch. Give me the potatoes.

— You can't carry all that.

— It's only two blocks.

— I should have given him some juice.

— Give me the onions then.

— You go on ahead. I'll wait with him.

— It's too cold.

— It's only two blocks.

Nick thumps his heels in fury. Knows it's a hundred blocks of snow covered roadway, years and years of blocks, and his wheels stolen by some vegetables. Unfair, protests Nick, as snot and tears slick his face, make him radiant. He arches his back and howls, luminous with anger.

His parents stand looking down at him — angry, confused faces in the sky. A pair of second-rate, badly lit demigods.

— Jeez, what a kid.

— What a brat.

— Get up, Nick.

— Please.

With difficulty, Mahon bends down and plucks Nick up off the ground, setting him on his own two feet. Nick argues in an inarticulate wail, wobbling but upright, but when my father lets go my brother collapses to his knees like a man shot dead in a film. He slumps sideways, still protesting. Now my mother takes a turn. She abandons the stroller, tries to scoop up Nick who, in turn, flails at her with arms and legs until she retreats, nursing bruises. Behind her the stroller — plastic bags hanging off each handle — overbalances and goes crashing to the sidewalk, spilling groceries across the sidewalk.

— Shit, says my father and puts his head in his hands. My mother, adding her voice to Nick's wailing, ratchets around the sidewalk, snatching oranges out of the snow.

A man in a ski jacket comes by, asking pointedly if we need help. He looks at Nick, who is now an incandescent wire of rage melting snow with his shouts. Later, recounting the story, my mother will lean heavy on the word 'help,' spinning it, implying that what the man offers is anything but — that he means to let my parents know what kind of job they're doing, with their broken grocery bags and their miserable kid.

— It's only two blocks, my mother says, turning red, clutching packages to her chest, unable to meet the stranger's eye. My father says nothing, faces away up the street. The man in the ski jacket gives all four of us a look colder than the winter street, than the wind, than the freezer chests back at the grocery store. Then he scowls, conveying his distaste for the scene before him, for my father in his raggedy coat, for my scrambling, red-faced mother. With that off his chest, Mr. Ski Jacket walks away. He's a lucky man, Mr. Ski Jacket — no rogue oranges in his snow.

My mother reloads the stroller, her breathing turning snotty in a way all too familiar to anyone acquainted with her son. My father gathers up more grocery bags, hefting them like life sentences.

— What an asshole, he says, at last.

— How hard, my mother asks the sky, asks the snow. — How hard can it be to do a little grocery shopping?

Ø

Bear with us. In time Nick will find his feet. His eyes will be dried with a mitten. His nose wiped in the same way. Taking his mother's hand, Nick will consent to walk again, plodding down the street with snow encrusting his backside. My father will follow behind, laying his footprints over ours.

What will my father think — watching Nick, watching Maeve — waddle on down the road? Watching us turn into our street? Stop in front of our building? What does he think, watching us reach home?

I know what he thinks. He thinks: only two blocks after all.

Only two blocks. His face says so as he lifts the last grocery bag over the apartment threshold, stops, rests. He stands propped up against the door jamb, looking in at our winter light, our grey carpet. Nick wanders past, a cookie already in hand. Singing Daddydaddydaddy. Mahon's home. Mahon's castle. No longer just a motherland.

My father straightens his back and reaches out as my mother comes for the last of the groceries. Mahon steps over the groceries to get a hold of her. Wraps his arms around her. Holds her tight. Kisses her gently. Then, together, they close the door on the outside world.

MY FATHER SEEMS SET TO STAY. We don't question our luck. Even Nick recognizes his daddy for real and true: not a conquering hero but an under-stuffed armchair, just another piece of parental furniture. My brother climbs on my father, sits on my father, ceases to pay him real attention. Even my mother stops clutching at Mahon in the night, crying into his sharp shoulder. We settle in. Calm down. Play house.

Tonight, red streaks lash our living room windows. Traffic on St. Clair retreating, stranding us on our island of lamplight. Ikea Family Robinson. Outside, the snow changes to freezing rain and back again. Inside, Nick protests a life behind bars. My mother has instituted a 'cry-down.' In the wake of the upheaval my father brought with his guitar and suitcase, Nick must be taught again to put himself to sleep. And not a moment too soon.

— He's got to learn, my mother tells my father. Her teeth clench, her fists ball. Down here in mission control the monitors all go haywire, needles point to the danger zone. Nick's crying blows my mother's fuses. But still, she contends, he's going to learn. Her jaw juts, her shoulders square. She's ready to insist but my father fails to disagree. He only nods, presses the volume button on the television remote and the Leafs skate louder. Settles back to enjoy the toothsome clacking of blades on ice. — He *will* learn, my mother says, speaking to the side of my father's head, to the slow motion replay, to the window sparkling with tail lights. Nick wails on. The telephone rings. My mother waits a bit, then struggles off the chesterfield.

As she approaches the hall and the table with the phone, Nick's shouting increases in volume. No remote on that boy, no mute, no off. — Hello, says my mother, speaking as loudly as she dares.

— Put him on, that bad bastard, says the voice on the other end of the line.

chapter four

My mother's gut elevators. She knows this voice. And now my father arrives, hovering like a ghost. Through some magic, he has divined that the call is for him. My mother thinks fast, doesn't meet his eye. — No, she says, no one with that name lives here. What number are you calling?

There is a deep, appreciative laugh from the other end of the phone — a laugh that my mother fails to reciprocate. My father disappears again, drifting down the hall and into the bedroom. My mother cranes her neck to follow.

— Put him on, Maeve, says the voice.

— He's not here, says my mother. — Isn't he with you? She's a terrible liar. Or maybe she just doesn't care very much.

— Tell him, says the voice on the phone, tell him I've got his gear, his amp, his bloody Fender. Tell him, pick up the phone or somebody loses a string.

A click from the line in the bedroom. The extension, picking up. My father speaks, querulously but with a note of pleasure too. — Dave?

— You asshole.

A lot of nervous laughing from my father.

My mother stands in the hallway, listening to the laughter, to Nick's un-muted shouting, making faces at the wall.

— She said you weren't there, but I know you, man. I know you.

— You know me. Where are you?

— Still in Barrie, dude. We're all here. Wondering why you aren't, man.

A silence. Well, not so much a silence as a moment in which no one speaks. Thanks to Nick's spectacular background vocals, true silence is unattainable for everyone connected with our apartment. My mother's continued presence on the line in the hallway allows even the pounding of Nick's feet on the wall to be transmitted from Toronto to a motel on the outskirts of Barrie.

— Missed the family?

My father takes the American fifth.

Ø

My mother has hung up and gone to find Nick. The minute she opens the door, he stops crying. She finds him lying stiff and angry on the mattress, arms at his side, staring up at her. His eyelids hang drop-heavy with tears. Silver streaks in the dark. This boy spends half his time roaring with pleasure and the other half roaring with rage — paired halves of a whole that's already twice as much as my mother can manage. He needs two mothers. Twelve mothers. Twenty-four. Forty-eight mothers wouldn't be enough. But he only has this one. She knows she'll never do, but she sits down and takes him in her arms anyway. The baby books advise against this — well, the ones she's reading this week. Never surrender. Never give in. But this is a sweet moment for the two of them.

After a while my father comes and stands in the doorway, his phone call evidently over. His shadow reaches across the floor, makes as if to slip under Nick's bed and hide, but his voice, when he speaks, sounds even, pleasant. Neutral. Once again, my father plays poker with his sentences.

— Dave thinks he can re-book some of what we missed, he tells her. — Van's almost fixed.

My mother says nothing, only hums to Nick and rocks a little. Not clear who she's comforting.

— When do you leave? she asks at last.

My father says nothing. Leans against the door and watches the three of us in the shadowy room. My mother hums, croons a little frantically. Her rocking takes on an edge. For a musician's wife, she sure can't carry a tune.

My mother still waits for an answer. Me too. My father stirs in the doorway. Turns. Slides out of view, leaving behind only the rectangle of yellow light that marks the empty doorway.

Reappears before we can panic. Speaks at last.

— Never said I was going, he says.

My mother looks down at Nick, angelically asleep in her arms. Okay, I made that last bit up. Of course Nick is not asleep. Only exhausted. Squirms fitfully. Calls out Daddy Daddy.

— Make no promises, says my father. And then he really does vanish. My mother hears the electric blink of the television turning on, catches the rise and fall of the commentator's voice, the ebb and flow of the hockey game as regular as tides. She shifts Nick to her other knee to ease a back so bent I have to brace it with one foot. Nick protests, wriggles, gets comfortable on her lap.

She lets her forehead rest on his dark head, closes her eyes. And just is. She just is.

ø

The question needs to be asked — the big one. You know it. You fear it. Let me take a big breath.

Where do parents come from?

There. I had to ask. I really want to know. How are they made? How do they get here? Don't tell me fairy tales about a bed and four feet. I don't believe that crap. I know parents have nothing to do with hanky-panky, or fun and games. I'm pretty au courant with the facts of life and, quite frankly, parents just don't make the cut. Their genesis must be more prosaic. Abandoned on the doorstep. Spontaneously generated from mouldy cheese. Constructed with marshmallows and toothpicks on a rainy day?

I know you know, so tell me. What's their story?

ø

My father runs this morning like all the others. This morning he brings home a surprise for my mother. — Look what I found outside, he tells her, blocking the door with his shoulders.

My mother stands in the hallway dressed in sweatpants and a dirty T-shirt. This morning, we are more pregnant than ever, so her hair crackles; her skin itches. She feels like every joint in her lower body has been broken and reset, back to front. — What? she says, hoping he's got an armload of hothouse flowers, despite the cold, despite the season, despite the cost.

My father steps away from the doorway.

You wouldn't think my mother would be vain now, would you? I mean, why would she bother? My mother wears, by habit, a monster's body — pink-eyed, pouch-faced, lousy with children unborn and otherwise. Her nose shines red 'cause she's always a little sick. Always a little nervous so her lips chap. I suppose her face could count as a badge of honour — worn with quiet humility and no pride, only suitable out in public on parade days — but today's no parade day. Still, feet shuffle in the hall, beat a tattoo at the door. And, as my father steps from the doorway, my mother straightens up, smoothes her hair, sucks in her gut. Her gut, I say. Her gut? My gut walls won't contract, not even one millimetre. I need all that space. But still she tries. I hear the shifting of ribs, the creaking of timbers under stress. I put out my two fists, straining. Veins a-pop.

My father steps back, reveals his find: a shaggy head that dips, grins, a hand that swipes hair from eyes. My mother says: *Duncan,* feigns pleasure, then, suddenly, she's not feigning. — Look Mahon, it's Duncan. I hear real pleasure in her voice now. She lifts brows, mimics amazement for our benefit. She steps toward Duncan.

— Hey. How y'doing, says Duncan. Duncan holds out his hand. They do a complicated thing with fingers that my mother gets wrong. She giggles, does a little knee bend, turns her face away.

I don't know this Duncan, tall and shaggy. *We* haven't been introduced. Neither, obviously, has Nick, who wanders in, all diaper-droop and belly-scratch. He and I stare at this stranger in our hallway.

— Oh, it's been ... it's been a long time, hasn't it, says my mother. 'Long' she says. L-o-o-o-n-g. Vowel sound egg-shaped. Suits her.

— Since Mahon quit the store, says Duncan.

— That long, says my mother, looking at my father. She stresses the 'that' as if 'that' were the whole of her life. Certainly, 'that' is the whole of mine.

— Hmmm, says my father, looking suddenly, desperately bored.

I'm bored too; but still ... to collect these driblets of my parents' lives, these droplets. Table scraps. Me and Nick, mouths open, ears flapping. Listening. Learning.

Ø

Duncan comes in for a cup of tea. He follows my mother into the kitchen, slides shyly past her, coming to rest beside the microwave. Mahon stops, stands his ground in front of the cupboards. My mother can't move freely in the narrow slot of a room, has to ask him to pass her the brown betty. She smiles at Duncan while my father searches up high for the teapot, reaches down low for the teapot — he hasn't got a clue where she keeps the teapot. My mother points this out to Duncan, just in case he hasn't noticed himself, laughs, shakes her head at my father's ignorance, says, — Really, he *does* live here.

Sympathetic Duncan smiles, but my mother never catches the grin he sends her way. Nick has just spilled his juice. — Paper towels, she barks. My father can find those, has needed to use them often in the short time he's been back. He spins the rack, rips with a proper paternal authority. Makes me proud. He stoops, wipes, stands, looks like a basketball player as he shoots the hoop of the kitchen sink with wads of sodden paper. — Not the sink, shouts my mother, already lurching into a rearguard action. Duncan steps out of her way as she rolls, basketball-shaped herself, past him and toward the fridge. In one hand she holds Nick's cup, while pouring a practiced stream of juice with the other. — Don't spill this one, she hisses at my brother, passing him the cup. Nick takes it, glancing quickly at Duncan and then toward the sink where his mother has begun to lift sodden wads of paper into the garbage. With a tentative grin at Duncan, Nick performs a little trick he hopes will entertain. Inserting his nose and mouth into the cup's opening, Nick sucks air, creating a hermetic seal between flesh and plastic. To Nick's delight, the seal holds and allows him to lift his cup a few inches from the table. Mahon watches, mirroring Nick's grin. But Nick's success undoes him, widens his smile and breaks the seal. A second spill of orange juice runs like yolk across the egg white surface of the table. My mother turns away from the sink to find Nick swinging his feet over a widening pool. My mother looks accusingly at Mahon who tries to assume the required expression — concerned, stern, disappointed, resigned — until my mother throws the dishcloth at the liquid on the table. Droplets of orange juice spatter my family.

Duncan twists in the doorway. He won't look at Mahon or my mother. He looks instead at Nick, meets his eye by mistake, can't help his nervous grin. Conspiratorial by default.

The whistle blows on the kettle. Time out. Mahon wipes up the juice while my mother gets Nick's old drinking cup from the cupboard. The drinking cup has a spouted lid and represents a demotion for Nick. The boy knows it. He sits at the table, head down, feet hardly swinging, refusing to acknowledge the cup, refusing to look up, smile, laugh, do anything that's by definition Nick. My mother makes tea with her eye on all of us.

— Sugar? she asks Duncan. — Cream? It's only milk really.

Duncan takes both. He attends to his tea, leaning over a spare corner of the counter. He measures out his sugar carefully, a teaspoon at a time. He measures out a lot of teaspoons. My mother watches Duncan; I know she wants to tell him that's enough — every fibre of her wants to say so. That's enough, Duncan, 's not good for your teeth. You'll ruin your supper. Mahon stirs his tea and looks out the window. A silence not altogether comfy hangs over us all.

— I think I have some lemon, says my mother, at the same time as Mahon begins to speak. In the time it's taken to stir his tea, my father has decided to unburden himself of various opinions about a band, continuing some conversation that he and Duncan must have begun in the street, in the hall. Or started months ago, when they still worked together in the music store. What my father has to say takes a while, involves hand gestures, many complicated comparisons. Maeve shuts her mouth and watches him fixedly.

— So right, Duncan says, when at last my father finishes his lecture. Nods his head appreciatively. A little younger than Mahon, this Duncan. Wears jeans, hair made greasy by pushing fingertips. Eyes on my father. Avoiding my mother. Duncan stirs his tea with a ring-a-ding-ding. Nods knowingly. Mahon, inspired, begins again. New disc. Wanna get. Have you heard? Blah, blah, blah.

My mother sighs. She believes with an unshakeable faith that my father's head contains a receiver for a psychic pirate radio station. Whenever Mahon looks blank in the bank, glazes over in the grocery, my mother knows the station has recommenced broadcasting: attention, all boys. Tune in. Dial up. Mahon with his antenna out, listening to music reviews, previews of the latest releases, hockey scores. Everything he needs to know.

Duncan smiles, shuffles his feet, puts more sugar in his tea. Dares to glance at my mother. My father intercepts, interrupts his own monologue. — This is great, says Mahon. — Great to talk to you. He half turns, addresses himself to my mother. — Last person I expected to see, and there he was, just outside, says Mahon. Just passing by.

— Just passing by, says Duncan.

— Oh, says my mother, a little archly for my taste.

— Forgot you lived around here actually, says Duncan.

— Oh, says my mother, to different effect.

— 's great, Mahon says enthusiastically, obliviously, picking up his mug. — Great to see you again. Long time. I've been, well, I've been on the road. My father waves his mug in the air, gestures randomly, slops tea.

Duncan nods sagely, shaggy head up and down. I see Nick out of the corner of my mother's eye, but no one else sees him. He's slipped out of his chair, lurks under the table. He's finished his juice, feels good, and so chooses this moment to greet Duncan properly, busting from cover, running full tilt at an unprepared, unsuspecting, unguarded man.

A man drinking tea.

Nick has a head like a stone; Nick's stone head reaches crotch-level on a tall man. Duncan is a tall man — have I mentioned? Nick meets Duncan. In slow motion, then, for maximum effect. Duncan convulses forward, spews tea, drops mug, clutches groin, groans oh so deep like a sub woofer, an undersea shock wave of pure pain.

Ø

I love slapstick. I love a guffaw. A belly-deep ho ho ho. A chuckle. A chortle. A snort. But my mother has no sense of humour. Can't see the fun in things. — Nick! shouts my mother. — Nicholas! You've done it now, Nick. This time you're in big trouble. She shakes her finger as she speaks: In (shake), Big (shake), Trouble (shake).

Motherhood: one long, horrible cliché.

So Nick goes into lock-up. Here's a surprise: Mahon puts him there. Ma and Pa, acting in concert just this once. Nick in stir. Bars on the crib, fists on the bars. Rattle, rattle. Nick shouting: Warden ... Warden. (My translation.)

I say: Aw. I feel for you, Nick. Sure I do. A bum rap. A real bum rap. In the living room, Duncan sits, leaning sideways against the chesterfield's curved arm. He's smiling faintly, unconvincingly. — An accident, says Duncan, weakly, politely. Such nice manners for a man in agony. My mother sighs, shrugs, and nobody knows if she's confirming or contesting the point. She goes over, pulls up a chair and sits across from Duncan, almost knee-to-knee. Now, ready to speak, she leans toward him. Duncan flinches. He can't help himself — my mother can look like Nick sometimes. I've noticed. In the mirror, pot lids, the oven's darkened front.

— I'm sorry.

— No, no. Just a bit ... well, jumpy.

— I wanted to offer you more tea.

— No, thank you, says Duncan.

— Something else then? I have some ... My mother has to think, has to run through the idiosyncratic contents of her cabinets. God knows what she'd meant to offer him but whatever it was she hasn't any. — Ice?

Duncan closes his eyes in horror; he shakes his head. — I'm fine. Really.

— Tempra, then? I don't think we have Aspirin. It's children's but you could have a really big dose.

— I think ... I think I'll?... Duncan looks for something. He twists his head from side to side. — Have you seen my coat? he asks.

Duncan's coat hangs beside my father's coat, which hangs crookedly from the loose hook in the front hall. My mother gets to her feet. She clearly thinks Duncan intends to go home, but Duncan has more pressing needs. He hobbles over to his coat, pats pockets, finds his bundle. Mahon catches on sooner, knows Duncan better. Knows those gestures. Mahon leads the way down the hallway and into the kitchen. The fire escape door scrapes open. Mahon speaks to Duncan over his shoulder, tells him he can smoke out here.

By the time my mother gets into the kitchen, they're already on the fire escape. My mother moves over to the window. The glass is streaky with St. Clair Avenue dirt. Through the grime, she sees Duncan with his baggie. Duncan with his rolling papers. Mahon with the big, fat blunt.

Ø

— Mommy. Nick sounds penitent all the way down the hall and into the kitchen. A certain blubbery, broken quality to his voice distinguishes repentance from rage or fright. My mother is a connoisseur of baby cries. Nick rolls them; my mother savours them.

My mother fetches Nick, carries him down the hall and into the living room, patting and speaking. — Slowly, slowly, gentle, gentle, she repeats to Nick, whose legs begin to work far in advance of the floor, kicking to and fro in anticipation of his sprint for freedom. She sets him down, and watches him race away. He's back in less than a minute, with a stuffed mouse, all broken nose and one eye missing. The mouse lunges toward her, the plastic ball of the nose sharply rapping her brow bone. My mother hugs the mouse anyway. She hugs Nick too, his small body half willing, half resisting. A familiar feeling. Nick, released, runs away. My mother hears bare feet on the kitchen floor and the smart rap of mouse nose on windowpane. She smiles to imagine Mousie's uncanny levitation as seen through the fire escape window. Duncan startled by rodent eyes in darkened glass. A double take. A choking cough. A sudden exhalation of blue smoke.

∅

Nick and my mother have decided to watch a video while Mahon entertains Duncan on the fire escape. Not that Nick rests — oh no. He shifts, wiggles, slides from chesterfield to floor and back again, only his eyes unmoving, fixed on the paintbox screen. Porky pink. Carrot orange. Bugsy grey.

After a while, Mahon and Duncan come back inside. My mother hears them come back into the kitchen: voices, chair scrapes, a deep bark of laughter from behind the half shut door. She means to get up, she wants to go join them, but she feels sleepy propped up against the chesterfield She swallows and refocuses her blurring vision on cartoon creatures with their knowing animal faces, their twisted mouths, their hard voices and rough accents. Trying to pay attention, to wake herself up. Oh, those three-fingered hands, those swollen heads. With effort, she tries to follow the story, but something slides out of whack. Rabbits and pigs turn up everywhere. All over the room. 2D rats, mice. Rabbit babies now, hopping off the screen. Long-eared babies in diapers. Grey babies with powder puff tails. Dog-tailed babies. Mer-babes meeting fishy ends. Centaur babies, difficult to diaper. Fat, dimpled cupids. Mythological babies spouting prophesy. Babies fibbing. Babies with forked tongues. Babies with no tongues. Babies with silver eyes. Babies with flippers. Feathered babies who caw like crows. Babies who fly in murders. Flapping babies, thin and black, lifting into the clear, cold sky over our apartment. Flying away.

Gerbil babies who dig and pry. Who take up residence. Who press into arch of brow bone, peer out through round window. Spit. Rub. Peer again. Who turn back to the jelly dessert of your brain, saying something you can't make out. Who sigh. Who roll their eyes.

Ø

Duncan knocks on the door frame, interrupts my mother's nap. He's in the hall, coat, hat on his head, going home already. Hell of a social occasion, thinks my mother as she picks herself up off the floor, fat and groggy. Duncan rocks, slightly, nervously grinning his apology for presuming to tap-tap while my mother slept. When my mother looks over at him blearily, he thumb-ups in her direction, as if to say: *My balls are good; don't you worry yourself about the state of my testicles.*

My mother smiles weakly, and Duncan is gone.

Ø

The sound of the door behind Duncan wakes my mother up properly. The minute he's really gone, my mother picks a fight with Mahon. — Well, she says, that was humiliating.

— What do you mean? asks my father, confused.

My mother can't be bothered to explain, looks tragic instead. — Everything in my life is crap, she says, pressing her fingers to her face.

My old man begins to take offence, scowls at her sideways. — Don't, he says, all uncertainty gone. He knows where she's headed.

— It's bad enough without witnesses.

— You were happy to see him.

— I was embarrassed.

— Tea? says father, in a falsetto voice, fluttering his eyelashes. I can't help but notice how his eyelashes are longer, prettier than my mother's.

Her turn now. — Don't.

— Don't you, he says in disgust and begins to imitate her again. — My life is crap, he says, in high-pitched and doleful tones, making a rubbing gesture with his forefinger and thumb. Hey. I recognize that sign: the world's smallest violin. How did he — ?

— Well it *is* crap. My mother shouts now. — It *is* crappy. In fact, it's *shitty*. Do you know how tired I am of being broke, living in this stupid apartment, never going anywhere? And with that, my mother begins to cry, turning her head so Nick can't see her. Nick steps around her, looks up curiously.

— You got that right. My father reaches up to grab his coat from the hook by the door, the loose hook as it happens. In his irritation he tugs too hard, removes both coat and hook from the wall. The hook, trailing screws, flies across the narrow hall and into the living room where it hits and shatters the mug my mother incautiously has left on the table. Lifting her head, my mother points hard at the mess.

— See, she says, though tears. — Crap.

In a cartoon we could count on bursts of steam from my father's ears, a high-pitched pressure whistle, maybe a bit of levitation off the grey carpet. Instead, Mahon turns red, appears to choke. Then he drops his coat where he stands and fires off down the hall. A second later, the crack of a drawer yanked open and shoved closed comes from the bedroom. Nick wanders down the hall to learn more but soon finds himself pushed aside by my father's legs striding back up the hallway. Mahon drops an envelope full of money into my mother's hands.

— What's this?

— It's for you. You can fix everything. Fix it all.

— But what is it?

— It's the door from Barrie, Maeve. Just the one night. Just one.

— Yes. But why do you have it?

My father looks at my mother. Too late he sees the trap he's set himself. My mother looks down at the money, back at my old man, catches on. What's the phrase: my father has the grace to blush? Except that he doesn't. He starts to laugh instead.

— You guys were playing for the *door,* says my mother, more scandalized by that than by my father's theft.

My father stops smiling. — Just some of the time ... Dave figured we'd make more doing our own booking.

— Oh god, says my mother, rubbing both her eyes with her fingers. She lifts her head and steps forward, taking the envelope from my father. She counts the money inside the envelope, flicking each bill with practiced fingers. Doesn't take long.

— That's it?

My father shrugs. My mother eyes thieving Mahon, starts to breathe so hard I fear for my rafters, for my roof tiles. I hang on to my hat. Hyperventilation with a chance of showers. She waves the money under his nose

— And he still wants you back after this.

My father doesn't answer for a bit. When he speaks I can hardly hear him. — Band knows we need the money. Knows I'm good for it.

— Stupid me, says my mother. Stupid, stupid me.

My father seems to speak to himself more than to her, whispering. — Just wanted to see you. Just wanted ...

— You never meant to stay, did you? All this time you knew you were leaving.

My father turns red again, goes grim, angry. — And you have no idea, he tells her, how *good* that felt.

He turns his back to her. They stand like that. Look at them there: Mom and Dad. My parents. Dumb kids.

DÉTENTE.

My mother lies awake in bed, only partially in the grip of a dream of something thin and papery. She presses my rooftop with fluttery touches. But I'm a bit preoccupied. I'm trying out a kind of intrauterine Braille, reading wallpaper and easy chairs. I slide my hands around my apartment ever so gently. I don't want my mother to feel me moving. Recently I've had to keep my knees, my elbows increasingly to myself. My room is getting snugger. Passages and halls I always meant to explore are too small for me now, closed forever. I'd looked forward to seeing those rooms. Now I'm readjusting, remeasuring, sliding my hands on the inside. Outside, my mother's hands do their own sliding. Moving. Slowing. Almost by accident our hands meet, touch through cell layer after cell layer after cell layer. No shock of recognition. No pressure or heat. But curiously her hands stop as if she feels me there, lurking, keeping as still as I can. I curl up tight, squinch up my eyes, go into free fall. Not-so-free fall as I hit the side of an armchair, sprawl backward over the coffee table. Slapstick Gerbil. My mother smiles.

My father is in our breadbox kitchen with the gingham floor. He's making familiar sounds. Cupboard doors bang. A drawer rattles. Coffee perks. Toast burns slightly. Nice, I guess, these domestic touches. Nick pipes himself into the kitchen soundscape with an ultrasonic question. My father rumbles in response. The fridge opens with an audible pop; a glass clicks on tabletop. The sticky glug-glug of apple juice. Out of the Tetra Pack. Into Nick.

A moment later the padding of my brother's feet tends this way. My mother rolls her eyes, but doesn't really mind. Nick comprises her area of expertise. She holds an advanced degree in Nicholas. And here comes her special topic now, flying through the air toward her. She holds out her arms for him, preventing an

chapter five

uncontrolled landing. Hugs him with a careful ardour. Now see me, Gerbil, pulling my hands in disgust from the walls, wringing my wrists, shaking Nick from my fingers like dishwater. I liked mornings better when she fought him off, lay stiff and unyielding, whined herself — anything other than exposing me to the embrace of my brother. I'm only inches away from the kid's grubby paws. He snorts and sniffles, laughs when my mother laughs. I can hear him nose breathing.

Get off me, I say. Get offa me. Get off.

A while later my mother yawns, leaves my brother stunt-driving little metal cars up and down a closed circuit course of sheets and duvet. Slipping quietly from the warmth of the bed, she makes for the living room, just visible at the end of the hall and glowing with a soft, grey light. She pulls up a blind and *ahhhs*. Outside, snow falls. Flakes cover up the coloured squares, the bright rectangles of city life, reducing St. Clair to a sketch, a streetscape of frigid pencil lines — thin at the horizon, detail collecting in the shadows, in the places where snow drifts. My mother rubs sleep from her eyes.

Down the hall, the shower starts up. My father begins to sing, softly. Snatches of songs, some his own. Elbows on the windowsill, mother begins to hum too, not the same tune — not really any tune at all — but nevertheless steadily and happily. The world is all right. For once. For now. So cue the unfurling streamers of solace, spilling like a wind-snatched scarf. Call forth the fireworks of satisfaction, those melting sparks transient as snowflakes. Let's hear it for domestic bliss. Unfashionable. Inexplicable. Incredible.

I could warn her, but she knows. She knows how it never lasts.

Ø

She bores me, my mother. Sometimes I drift off. Yes, I do. Long moments of inaction, cow-like rumination of no interest to anyone but herself. She's a snooze-fest, my old lady. My bed tempts me always, soft and absorbing and warm. A nourishing bed with muscular sheets, fleshy pillows, lulling me deeper and deeper, singing me back to sleep with thighs and bellies and breasts.

I'm awakened by the usual silly fuss to an unusual degree: my mother running around in a dirty shirt and flapping shoe laces, no time for her own torso, her own feet. She chases Nick, who wears nothing but a diaper and a red face. He screams bloody murder: freedom's clarion call. — Leb me go. Leb me go. He runs and screams. Pauses while my mother leans against the wall to catch her breath. Then she screams and runs herself until she catches him at last and grimly folds him into a shirt. Stuffs him into pants. Slots him into socks. Says: Jesus, Nick, will you please shut up.

— Here, says my father from the end of the hall. Behind him popcorn puffs of steam drenched in golden light shoot from the open bathroom door. In his towel and buttery sheen, he's a vision, my father. Daddy to the rescue. He calls: Nick, get over here, buddy. And, as part of his effort to evade our mother, Nick comes immediately. Mahon bends, reaches out to his son, but my brother has no intention of playing anyone's game save his own. He avoids our father's arms and instead dives headfirst into Mahon's bare feet. Mahon looks down in surprise at his son, who begins to savagely tear at his own socks. Nick has assumed the furrowed expression of a Dark Lord well versed in foul deeds. He mutters arcane syllables, prescriptions of incipient violence. Despite a fair warning from the kid, Mahon bends down, scoops up both Satan and his socks. Clearly our father intends to charm Nick, to magic him out of malevolent bad humour and back into his clothes. But wicked Nick won't play rabbit to Mahon's hat. Struggling with increasing violence, Nick tears at buttons, bucks backward out of pants. His flailing foot knocks my father's towel loose, kicks the socks from his hand. Mahon grabs for a sock, trips on his towel, loses his grip on Nick. With an evil wail, Nick begins to slip from my father's grasp.

A flourishing thicket of parental arms blossoms around Nick. Nick lands in its embrace, thorns and all.

Ø

My parents face each other in the living room. Nick wears clothes but only just. So does Mahon. Nick, restored to our father's arms, cries steadily, covers their T-shirts in snot.

—Are you sure you can do this? asks my mother, raising her voice to be audible over Nick's sobs.

Mahon doesn't answer, chooses to look hurt at the question.

My mother shakes her head. —I just don't know if this is the best....

—Go, go, my father interrupts. Shuts her up by meeting her eye. Shows her he means what he says.

And I mean what I say. I say: they'll be fine, Mom. So go on. (Whatever.)

—Go, Maeve, says my father again. —You need a break before I ... you need to get out.

Out?

My mother looks at my father, who sets Nick down on the living room floor. My brother, unleashed, runs toward my mother and wraps himself around her knees, a baby snake on his first morning at the python daycare. Now he screams, my brother. Not cries. Not whimpers. Screams. Imagine straining jaws, fangs, forked tongue, an unnatural voice: shrieking. Unnatural? Unholy, more like.

—You're right, says my mother. —It's a last chance to get, y'know ...

Out?

Ø

Out.

Late winter's winds and puffs of frantic, last-minute snow. Actual snow. Actual weather. Not through a window. Not on the television news. Cold seeps in through the cracks in my mother. She's even less well-made than I thought. Drafts up back staircases I never knew existed, under weatherstripping I'd never noticed. Is she made for this, my mother? Is this really all right? Light leaks in under her lids, through her lashes. A bright whiteness that comes not from the sky but from under the layers of snow, from inside the landscape's heart.

Ding-ding. Streetcar rings its bell, slows and stops. My mother climbs inside and the cold stops. The brightness stops.

Thank god for insides. Insides belong to Gerbil — my sort of thing. Just think, I'm inside this streetcar. I'm inside my mother — my fleshy Styrofoam bash and bang protector. I'm packed up tight by the front bumper of her, but make no mistake, I find nothing personal in these entirely biological precautions. Protecting me, safekeeping precious Gerbil — not something she does with her brain. No way. My mother pokes her big belly at edges, corners, sharp projections. She pushes me forward, saying, excuse me, excuse me. What, I wonder, did she do that she needs to be excused so much? Rhetorical question.

But, still, I treasure insides — I'm something of a connoisseur. And safe inside, I can think about outsides. Poke my nose not exactly out, but far enough to catch the tang of winter coats. The exhaust-plume smell of our street, car-clogged and choked with buildings. The odourless stink of the long, grey sky. Outsides. Drawn (not quartered, never that). Published — a revised edition. Read by a yawning medical student reviewing her anatomy text. Outsides, page 273. Inner workings of. Diagram of. See page 274 (a longitudinal section with interior organs outlined and coloured cartoon pink). Overleaf, page 275. Cross-section of. Pregnancy in. Oddities of. And wait. Something familiar, uncovered, exposed, tucked into a living room, with a hand out the window and a foot up the chimney. Jammed in tight and blinking, stupid in sudden daylight. Outside pours in.

Outside won't quit. Our streetcar begins to move, passes our apartment (page 276), which rises, recently cross-sectioned by our exit. Inside, there's a mess: tattered wallpaper, twisted wire, plaster, steel rods, pipes severed by the scalpel cut. The whole street filled with dust and debris, filled with cascading brick. Up in the jagged wound of our living room, Mahon and Nick wave goodbye, uneasy in each other's company. Down below, my mother pretends she can't see them, sits with her hands on her knees. No one sits beside her. An entire block of storefront will pass by before my mother allows herself to smile. No Nick crawling, crapping, crying. Out.

Block after block of buildings. The streetcar goes on and on, leaving behind its gleaming incision in the road.

Ø

My mother's pleasure makes me sick. She couldn't care less about my discomfort, grins herself from stop to stop. Eagerly she looks out the window as the streetcar slides into the ground, taking us to a subway train. We climb inside this subway car, which, in turn, shoots itself into a vein in the earth. All this should invigorate me, renew me, stoke me with the insideness of everything. No go. Light and cold seep in through the gaps in my mother's smile, slip between the white stones of her teeth. Over my head, blue vapours collect, swirl, drop through my mother's dim core. They find me, those tendrils of outside, ruffling my fur with their chilled breaths. And I know I'm far away from that familiar strip of St. Clair, safety-netted by a web of wires, by leaning poles, by street lights. When I look out again, my mother no longer rides the subway, but now mounts stone steps up to a thin skin of pavement. She puts her boots on its surface, plants her feet in the thick slush that covers it. Her feet root ceiling-side, her head hanging dangerously, carelessly into the depths of the sky. Up or Down. In or Out. Gerbil's brain hurts. Gone are the familiar shop fronts, the brick battlements of home, windowed with easy eyefuls of cloud. Gone are apartment walls, buttressed by Nick's shouting, by his roof-raising yells. Outside blows wide open. I'm spattered by air, by oxygen. Buildings jump back, sidewalks lift. Sky contracts — a pupil in sudden sun. A fist clenching. A heart contracting.

Ø

Here's something I don't get. In the end we spend little time unmoored outside. Something about the sky begins to bother Maeve, takes the edge off my mother's pleasure. She gazes at the absence over her head, pretends to take deep breaths of nothing. Then she flees, turning into the first coffee shop she can find.

My mother finds a chain with its easily recognizable logo and rocking, uneven tables. She sits down in the window with a grapefruit juice and a goitre-like muffin. The muffin tastes sweet, feels sticky, crumbly, difficult to remove from its paper coat. Maeve eats half and pushes the other half to the edge of her tray, wiping her fingers on a napkin. The grapefruit juice tastes cold and unpleasant after so much sweetness. Also, my mother has not chosen her seat well. The window seat, which at first seemed to her like a sit-and-be-seen sort of seat, turns out to be a sit-and-be-frozen sort of seat. The door opens again, and my mother puts her coat back on. She's begun to shiver despite the blast furnace that is yours truly. Behind her, more comfortable looking tables stretch along a sexy naked-brick wall. Under golden halogens more competent customers talk in low voices, read papers, work on laptops. Not far away, students push their books aside in order to laugh all the harder. In the back corner, an earnest-looking man with long, black hair and glasses clearly revises his novel: a witty page-turner, profound but with an immense popular appeal. A literary best-seller and ... and ... Maeve begins to snivel, wondering 'readible?' 'Readeble?' Able to read? My mother fusses about her brain, wishes she'd brought a book. Gets up, deciding to buy one.

My mother finds a bookstore just around the corner. Hey, Mom. Listen up. Once upon a time there was a fat, lonely woman who lived just off a stretch mark of a street. Spring might have been coming but it certainly hadn't arrived yet.

One day, while she was out shopping, she wandered into a magic bookstore where she bought — what else? — nothing. She wandered for ten minutes up and down the aisles, unable to find anything to read. Unable to make even the slightest decision. What the hell's the matter with me? thought the fat, lonely woman.

— Are you finding what you're looking for, says a pleasant young man. His smile alarms her, vaporizes her social skills.

A hermit comes down off the mountain, a novice escapes from the convent, a shipwrecked sailor spots a sail — these re-entries demand our attention, our sympathetic engagement. I'm here to tell you my mother's case is hardly as intriguing as the least of these. I give my mother a kick in the ribs. She grunts, finds her voice. — I'm good, she says, although that's hardly the point. The young man smiles again, claims to be available if she needs him. He takes himself over to the cash desk, where he attends to a stack of paper. My mother watches him from behind her hair. She sees him taking calls and ringing up sales. How nice to work in a bookstore, she thinks to herself. I think: this is stupid, my mother. You couldn't work in a bookstore. How could you? You don't read anymore. You open books; you see Nick coming; you sigh; you put them down again. What do you know about books, about reading — about content? Outsides, oh yes — you know faces and backs and spines. But what do you know about the inside of what other people do all day? About cash? Desks? Stacks of paper? Phone calls? Sales? Gerbil wants to know, Mother.

My mother gives her head a little shake as if to deny everything. She frowns, picks up a book at random, and opens it to Chapter One. Reads "I am a sick man.... I am an angry man. I am an unattractive man." She bursts into tears.

∅

My mother calls home. She's been on her own for an hour and a half. Time for a fix.

The phone rings just once. Snatched up.

—'Lo

—Mahon?

—Why are you calling? What's the matter?

—What's the matter there?

—Nothing's the matter here. Where are you?

My mother tells him. She's been to a coffee shop, been to a bookstore. She misses them. Asks to speak to Nick.

—He's napping, says Mahon. Casually. As if this weren't a miracle.

—Napping? My mother sounds almost outraged.

—We had a snack ... we were singing together ... I dunno. He just went down. I just hope the phone didn't.... Fully ten-tenths of Mahon's concentration is focused elsewhere.

—Mahon?

—Ummm?

—You're not listening to me.

—What? Oh, thought the phone might have woken him.

—He's really asleep?

—Well, now I don't know. Obviously.

—Go check.

—What? Listen. Maeve. If he's not awake now, he will be then.

—What if he's not asleep.

—I'd hear him.

—No. I mean what if he's not asleep. Not. *Asleep.*

—Not. *Likely.*

My mother grimaces over the telephone, frightens passersby. Gives the command. —Just check him.

Maeve waits on the phone while my father's footsteps dwindle and disappear. She's just inside the front doors of a big downtown store. Noisy. She puts one hand over her phone-less ear and listens. Quiet. A rustle and my father is back on the line.

— He's out, Maeve. Didn't even stir when I opened the door.

— Is he breathing. Did you ...

— He's breathing. He's sleeping, Maeve. He's fine. He's just sleeping.

Spoken like my mother needs bright syllables, block-shaped. My mother toys with her coat. — Well, if you're sure, she says at last.

— Maeve. This getting out thing...

— Uh-huh?

— A really good idea.

Ø

The museum looms grey on grey. Stone and windows. My mother visits often with Nick. This is what she tells people: not many people appreciate how prepared big museums are for people like Nick: Plate glass, display cases, frequent bathrooms. Art galleries don't welcome Nicks. Art galleries hang priceless works down low, set ceramic sculptures on narrow bases, create tempting installations easily destroyed by fingers darting out at stroller height. Before she knew this, Maeve and Nick closed a show or two. Museums, on the other hand, provide room to breathe — big, old-fashioned galleries that no one ever enters. Thank god, thinks Maeve, for the Forgotten Galleries. Thank god for the worn carpet pathways, the burnt-out bulbs, the blank and broken computer displays. Thank god for these streaky glass bolt holes. And my mother, a fat homing pigeon, waddles up the stairs and finds herself in amongst the trilobites, the dusty swamp display, the Rocks of the Precambrian Shield. She finds herself — a sad, round lump — sitting in front of the tall, glass cases, where Nick likes to run full-throttle at his reflection, and where no one ever stops him. She subsides into a mood (a puddle?) of quiet retrospection. Nick. Mahon. Her. Me.

Someone surprises my mother there, in front of a display of replica mammal-like reptiles — hell, surprises me too. I long to be introduced to the young lady in the heels and skirt-suit. The shapely female who goes in where my mother goes out. Well? Gerbil's waiting. — Maeve? The stranger speaks with more than an assumed astonishment. She really is amazed. — Is that you?

My mother looks up. Focuses. Sees a face from long ago. Several years anyway. Before Nick, for sure.

— Marie-Claude?

Marie-Claude possesses real poise. Marie-Claude swivels her hips, only smiles when my mother begins to rave. — Oh my god. Oh my god. I can't believe it.

— But what are you doing here, Maeve? You are working?

— Working? Oh no. I'm just taking ... some time.

— Some time? Oh, yes. I see. (She does not.)

My mother gets heavily to her feet. Sways.

— But you are going to have a baby, says Marie-Claude.

— Oh yes, says my mother, delighted to find something positive to say. — I am going to have one. Another one. I mean I already have one — a brother. Not this one. This one isn't the brother. This one is the other. The other other one is the brother. He's not here, the other other one. Just this one. But not yet, of course.

Marie-Claude looks a little bewildered by this, but smiles. — Two, she says.

— Two, says my mother.

Head shaking ensues. Two babies. What a wonder.

— Are you? begins my mother, unsure of where she's headed conversationally. — Do you? What are you?...

— Oh, just a fellowship, says Marie-Claude. — Late nineteenth-century works on paper. Perhaps a small show too. I'm thinking of a few things. Canadian mostly. The prints are very brittle; the originals have done better. Green. Löki. Tremblay too. Marie-Claude giggles.

— You're working here? my mother asks stupidly. She'd thought she was safe here.

Marie-Claude looks at her hard. — Yes, she says at last. — That is, in the archive.

My mother's discomfort differs from cramp, heartburn, indigestion. The pain hits her in the same place, but she knows it's nothing physical.

— And when? asks Marie-Claude smoothly, stretching out her finger tips — pale crescents. She reaches but doesn't touch. — When does this one arrive? What is his exhibition date? She smiles.

— Her, says my mother. An instant. A reflex.

— You know then. A girl.

— No, says my mother. — I have no idea really.

— A feeling, says Marie-Claude with another smile. — The famous mother's intuition. A girl to go with the brother. With?

— Nick.

— Yes. A matched pair. A set. We will put them on display here, in the museum. The Babies of Maeve. Lineups around the block. Marie-Claude laughs again. Then her face grows serious. — And afterwards ... what will you do?

— Afterwards?

— After the baby? When you are no longer 'taking some time'? You will go back to work, yes?

— I am working, says my mother. — I'm working all the time.

Marie-Claude sets herself right, utters statements not questions. — Yes, of course you are. It is very good work that you do. Very important work. You are happy with this work. You choose it.

— No, says my mother, my disagreeable, my perverse mother. What's the matter with her?

— No?

— I mean, I chose once upon a time. I just didn't ... Maeve pauses, then says in a rush, — Staying home, Marie-Claude, it's like being dead. And my mother makes a terrible face, frightening

Marie-Claude every bit as much as Marie-Claude's suit frightens my mother. The two of them take a step away, then a step toward each other, groping for shoulders, elbows. Sisters at a scary movie. Yieee!

— But Maeve ...

— No, I did choose. I really did.

— You are an educated person. You have degrees, options.

— Options?

— Your husband?

— No, see, there it was my choice. My idea.

The women drop arms, step back. I personally find it odd that my mother isn't crying. She's dry-eyed — out of character. Brave for Marie-Claude? No. She just isn't sad.

— They are lucky children, says Marie-Claude.

My mother shakes her head, as well she might. We both think of days she does nothing but complain, days she does nothing but shout. I think of my mother: inconsistent, volatile, unhappy, selfish, stubborn, self-pitying, immature, neurotic ... should I go on? I could, you know. I could fill pages.

— No, she says, I really don't think so.

Marie-Claude shrugs. — Well, perhaps you don't know.

My mother laughs at this. — Oh sure. I don't know anything. That much I know, she says. Can I come to your exhibition when it opens? *Your* baby — if that's not too much of a cliché?

Marie-Claude appreciates this, nods vigorously. — I will send you an invitation to the opening. And you will buy a wonderful dress. I think you will not be so ... She gestures with her hands, adding a well-manicured bubble of air over her own midriff.

— Won't last forever, agrees Maeve.

— And do you know what I think, Maeve?

— What?

— Forgive me, but I want to say this ...

— What?!

— I think you look like you need to get out more.

Ø

My mother spends the rest of the afternoon wandering amongst the furniture collections, looking in at imaginary rooms filled with real beds, tables. She wonders where the baby slept, where you put all seven children, how you stood it way back then. When she has had her fill of antique desperation, her own late-model, mass-produced, semi-disposable angst has lifted enough for her to catch the streetcar home.

St. Clair — the once and future incision site — is bright in the early evening darkness. I'm exhausted by outsides, keep my head safely tucked under my tail, curled up tight with my back to the world. My mother leans her head up against the darkened glass, looks forward to home, to her boys. I'm as small as I can go — the insider, the ghost in the machine. St. Clair slips into my dreams: the oversized houses layered with doctors', and dentists' offices give way to milk stores, each with a backlit flag of chocolate bar convenience. Children's clothes, hardware stores, greengrocers iron-grilled against the night. Lit signs glow blue and yellow, red and green. Windows reflect our car, rattling homeward.

And over it all, a gibbous moon. Well, no moon, really. Made that part up. Over it all, stars, I guess, trying to pierce the city's orange nighttime haze. A moon? I don't really know, can't be bothered to find out. Only thing moon-like I can see is my round mother, floating home with a smile between puffed, pale cheeks. Oh mother. Oh Maeve.

Apartment dark when Maeve gets home. She nods appreciatively at the air of quiet stillness from the darkened windows. Nick down already, she fervently hopes, and the thought doesn't cause the slightest stir of professional jealousy. Wants Mahon to cope, my mother does. Doesn't begrudge him this morning's nap or an early bedtime. Doesn't mind if he's reading right now, or listening to music on the headphones. Even imagines herself and Mahon on a quiet chesterfield, quite alone except (she neglects to think) for me. Maeve takes out her key at the bottom of the stairs, climbs the stairwell dim and still, devoid, for once, of thudding bass lines or other people's party noise. The lock of her apartment door turns easily in her hand and she enters, calling softly: Mahon. Mahon?

Daddy?

She finds my father in the bedroom. Nick lies on his stomach on the bed, watching Mahon move about the room. Half asleep, my brother kicks his legs to keep himself awake. As my mother enters he gives her a look as if to say, you again, and turns his attention back to his father. Mahon opens a drawer, looks inside.

— Thought I'd let him stay up.

My mother leans against the dresser.

— You were longer than I thought, says Mahon, with a handful of socks. He seems to be focused on laundry, hasn't looked fully at her yet.

— Well, says my mother. — I had a good time.

— Okay, says my father. — Good. He speaks carefully, neutrally. He looks at the socks in his hand. Looks up at my mother. Meets her eye.

— You were right, she tells him. Smiles.

My father doesn't speak.

— Getting out, y'know. You get a bit of perspective. I feel stronger. Better.

My mother comes over, stands at the end of the bed. She watches Mahon pile more socks on the bed, sees him pick up a stack of shirts. For the first time, she takes in the suitcase that lies open on the bed beside Nick. Another new perspective.

Determines not to cry.

ALL ACROSS THIS CITY, men wash out diapers, make breakfast, croon singsongs to happy boys while sunshine slants though kitchen windows. But not in our house. In our house, the kitchen sits silent, diapers ripen. No one sings in our house. In our house, we're missing my old man's Gretsch, a spare diaper bag stuffed with clothes. We're missing my father's running shoes, his hat. We're missing footsteps, whistles, clunks, and thuds from another room. We're missing a big chunk of what we were yesterday.

One of us might go after Mahon if chasing were an option, but we're hobbled, my mother and I. I'm her ball and she's my chain. She's my dungeon, my windowless cell. I scrape at her walls, rattle my tin mug against her bars. I shout for the warden, but when the warden comes she wears my mother's sad face, her frown, her cracked voice. *Out?* says the warden, if only I knew how.

Do I sound a little hysterical? *Husterikos.* We all know that word's storied past, linked to my changeable home. Who would blame me — young as I am — if, from time to time, my emotions escaped my novice control and my rodent face crumpled, then cried — if my tiny body were wracked by un-suppressed misery? But Maeve, not Gerbil, is the hysterical one. Exhibit A: my mother heaving and sobbing and crying until breath comes in gasps. Watch her now, weeping beneath the dining room table. She sits on the floor with legs out in front of her and lets the tears and snot come willy-nilly. Look at her there. Let's recall her own words: *stronger. Better.* Ha. The woman has no resilience; perspective is exactly what she'll never acquire. She blubbers into her hands until her nose swells and reddens, until her eyes puff, until her lip crenellates. Her sobs well up from deep inside her — deeper even than me. Her lamentations shake my walls and rattle my skull until my teeth chatter in my head. *Mother,* I tell her patiently. *This is too much.* Dramatics. Self-indulgence. Hysterics. Stop it; stop now.

chapter six

Unflaggingly, I repeat myself. But between the sound of my clattering teeth and the fluid in her ears, nothing gets through to her. Nothing. My mother snivels and whines, cries intently. She wipes her nose with the back of her hand, rubs her eyes with her knuckles. Sniffs. Measures the holes in her heart and begins to wail again.

She's been under this table all night. Couldn't bear to use the bed. Slept (sort of) on a floor padded with snatched pillows, a quilt freshly decked in dust bunnies. My tragic mother clutches a T-shirt of Mahon's, wet with tears, crumpled — no less than the skin under her eyes — by misery. What's a Gerbil to do? Pack my bags, lace up my boots, jam on my best straw boater? Take my place in the hallway with my finger on the switch, looking for the door? Search for the door? Wherever is the door?

No way out. Knew that.

I don't feel sorry for my mother, the misery-goat. My father left yesterday, but he called her as soon as he got in. Took longer than she wanted but not so long as all that. Snatched at the phone, put it to her face like an oxygen mask on Mars, sucking everything she could through those daisy holes.

— Mahon?

The line is good, crystal clear. Noise in the background, but Mahon's voice sounds in her ear just like he was curled up beside her, here on the floor under the dining room table.

— Just got in. My father sounds tired, not at all as elated as I think he should. — Dave met me at the bus station just like he said. We're all here. Motel. No vans. You know I told him.

My mother listens, soaking up the sound of his voice even though the sodden nature of her soul would hardly seem to admit another drop of sentiment. She presses the receiver to her ear and the background noise becomes meaningful, becomes insistent music. Sounds of voices calling, laughing. My mother puts a fluttering hand to her forehead, a heroine in a melodrama. Oh Me. Oh My. My mother suffers from an allergy to the undertone of satisfaction in Mahon's voice, suffers from the certainty that my father is relieved to be back on the road. The road: certainly dangerous, possibly fatal, and leading far, far away. But Mahon's satisfaction is transitory at best. Miles up the highway, Mahon's already sighing into the phone. Mahon sighs. — I'm here, he says. — I'm back on the fucking road.

Maeve chokes, coughs, snots, wipes, makes little incoherent cries (a laugh in fact, cleverly disguised). A panicked laugh, for she's troubled by what she wants to come next: the set piece of this telephone conversation. She will not be denied, has spent her waiting hours preparing her opening statement to the jury, rehearsing before the darkening shapes of chesterfield and chairs. In strangled sobs, she's made herself word perfect, practicing her list of charges, point by point. She's howled each item out to the empty apartment, every complaint strangely truncated by snivels and cries. *I was wron-on-ong ... Not stronger — not me-hee-hee ... I need you-hoo-hoo.* She's practiced over and over. Now she's tongue-tied, unable to begin. My mother's slate is blank.

— Maeve?

— ...

— You there?

Certainly she's here, still crying down the phone line. She's here gasping for words. For human speech (comes so easy to me). Despite all her rehearsing, she can't think how to start.

— You mad?

Oh yes. This too. She's kicked things, my mother — anything unwise enough to get in her way, like the edge of the chesterfield, the zombie dryer (still undead). She's yelled *you loser* into the bend of her elbow, her words muffled for Nick's sake. *You sad loser,* she's hollered in such a way that only the soft skin on the inside of her arm knows exactly what she said — except for me, of course, 'cause my ears are permanently pricked. My seat's a front row seat and there's no sidling out for popcorn. Still, just because

I hear her doesn't mean I *get* her. For example, who's the loser: her or my old man?

Trick question. Just checking, making sure you're still paying attention. Of course, there can only ever be one loser to Gerbil's mind: that sorry woman exercising her frustration by imagining a hole in the drywall in the front hall — a neat, little, toe-sized loser-puncture. She thinks very, very hard about this hole until she can feel the power of her swinging foot, the satisfying, powdery giving-way of the wall. An imaginary puncture, its dark outline utterly invisible in the half-light of the hall. Fantasy damage. *Famage. Damtasy.* Make-believe slashing, breaking, crushing, smashing, and — because it's only pretend — quite unlike the drawer she's dared to yank out, to leave lying on the bedroom floor (after all, even Nick can't hurt himself with a sock). The drawer exists in real life. It really lies upturned with all my father's left-behind socks spreading across the rug. Left behind, just like my mother herself, who knows herself one with the socks. Mad? She's just as furious as she dares.

— Maeve? Say something.

— ...

— 's not forever, Maeve.

My mother continues to consider the socks, inhales the phone deeply, as if she could suck my father home. But she breathes more evenly. Oxygen reaches her brain for a change. Makes a difference. A bit. She holds the phone away from her ear, motions to Nick who's been lurking in the dark of his bedroom, eyes gleaming. She gives him the receiver — what motivates this?

Nick looks at the phone in his hand, now seems uncertain as to what to do next, suspicious of being so easily given something for which he usually clamours in vain. Nick has a right to be suspicious, a pawn in an idiot game of chess. A rumbling query leaks down the phone line and into his hand. His father's voice. My mother tightens her grip on Nick who grips the phone in turn. Lifeline.

Nick puts the phone to his ear tentatively. I know what my father hears. Heavy breathing. Whistling boogers. — Nick, says my mother, say something to Daddy.

— Daddy, says Nick, and then, for some reason, the precious phone pops from his iron grip. Maeve and her son both scramble for the tumbling receiver. Snatch the cord. Bang heads. A moment of low comedy. I'm laughing; I'm no snob. A moment later, Nick, restored to the line, treats his father to more heavy breathing, this time with a sullen edge, a quavering-on-the-edge-of-tears edge. — Daddy? says Nick suspiciously. A silent tear slides down Maeve's cheek, dribbles from her chin as she watches Nick's face switch on. Oh, he's happy to hear Mahon's voice. To know Daddy's there at the end of the line. My mother clutches the telephone's base, leaves finger dents in the plastic surface.

— Dere's Daddy, Mommy, Nick says in an altered tone of voice. — Daddy's dere. Nicholas waves the receiver in the air.

— Talk to him, Nicky.

— Daddy? (To give my mother credit, she cringes at the next bit, although every word is her work as surely as if she'd said it herself.) — Daddy come home?

This is dirty pool. Bad Maeve. Naughty Maeve. You knew Nick would say something like this. You know your boy's mind, and he knows yours. After all, he's watched you cry, bite your arm, stomp your feet. The two of you, thrown together, day and night, minute after minute, second by second — a lack of perspective that brings a certain perspective. An inside-skinside certainty of the way each other's mind works. How dare you aim your son, point, fire.

Mahon rumbles on the other end of the line and Maeve can't make out a word. Now suddenly, unexpectedly, Nick laughs.

— What, Nicky? What did Daddy say? Maeve can't stop herself. She puts her own ear to the receiver, pulls it closer to her own. Who's sorry now, Mom? Huh? Nick struggles for the phone and Maeve, surprised, relinquishes the receiver. She reproves Nick with a glare, but my brother shows independent-mindedness. Puts the receiver firmly back to his own ear. Listens.

— Okay, says Nick to his absent father.

— Yes, says Nick, I tell her.

— Okay, Daddy, says Nick. — Good ...

— Nick! says my mother desperately. — Don't say it ... don't say ...

My mother fumbles for the receiver. This time she snatches, grabs, pulls.

— Bye, says Nick.

And my mother wrestles the phone away from her own flesh and blood, claps the receiver to her own ear, ignores Nick's loud protests. She calls Mahon's name down the line again and again until, at last, his self is summonsed back. — What's going on? he says in her ear.

— I, my mother answers. — I. She has to turn her back on the still-protesting Nick. He pounds her hard between the shoulders, recognizing a barrier when he sees one. My mother says 'I,' beginning her explanation, finds herself unable to speak under the assault of Nick's thudding. Aye-aye-aye comes out of her mouth, as Nick's fists turn her into a percussion instrument. Nick improvises a few bars. — You-oogh-oogh, says my mother. — Sto-ah-ah-ah-op. Nick gives a last whack (Ma-han, spits my mother) before he finally gives up and changes tack. Now he idly pounds the wall with his feet. At last, my mother, free to speak without rhythmic interference, cuts to the chase.

— I can't do this, Mahon. I can't do it again and again. My mother finds her voice, and it's a whiny, self-pitying one.

— I know.

— So don't tell me ...

— What if we make this the last time, Maeve? What if this is it?

Silence, except for Nick's feet keeping time, whacking the backbeat out of the walls. A musical family. Just not a happy one.

— I don't want to do it anymore either, my father says. A lyrical line over the percussion. Almost too delicate to be audible.

— What?

— Can't really talk about it now. I'll call tomorrow.

— Huh?

— I'll call every night.

My mother waits a beat, another beat, another. — Okay, she says at last.

Nick, sensing a shift, stops drumming with his feet, rights himself, and considers long and hard (three seconds max). He wants back on the telephone. My mother fends him off with an arm and, for a second, he disappears. He returns with Mousie in his arms and, without pausing to let her act first, raps the toy's cracked nose sharply against the mouthpiece. — No, Nicky, says my mother, fending off of Mousie with both arms, telephone receiver held fast between shoulder and clenched jaw.

— Nick talk to Daddy, he says in a determined voice.

— Nick? says my father. A cautious welcome.

— Nick, says my mother. A world of difference.

— Put him on again.

My mother passes over the phone. — Daddy, says Nick, between adenoidal gusts. My mother listens. Hears Mahon's monosyllabic encouragement, hears his expectant silence.

— Daddy?

Urging sounds from the receiver.

— Daddy?

Silence. Open, waiting, patient, fatherly, long-distance silence.

Next thing my mother knows, Nick is replacing the telephone handset on its base, tenderly, carefully — a boy putting a baby to bed. My father, far, far away, miles to the north, attached to the end of miles of wires hung pole by pole from this St. Clair apartment all the way to a strip of motels along a highway — my father hears Nicholas, the booger-king, disconnect. And it's over. He's gone. Absence knocks my father back down its throat with a chaser of silence.

What's Maeve doing now? Laughing? Crying? Something in

between. Don't ask me, down here in cellblock nine, in P4G, in the poke, because I don't know. I'm still stuck here, underneath the dining room table, wrapped in a dusty quilt and an early morning sunbeam. We've had hours to play this call over and over in our twin memory banks, in our separate heads, but still Maeve can't make up her mind. Laugh? Cry? Be of two minds?

If only.

Ø

Count the days by sleeps. Count the days by peanut butter sandwiches. My mother stands at the kitchen counter and sniffles into jars, into boxes, into plastic bags filled with whole wheat crusts. In this way she salts our food, this Queen of Burnt Toast. Our Lady of the Crusts.

The kettle wails, joins in the general dismay of our little household. My mother makes tea, sets herself and her mug down at the little metal table. Pale sunshine slips into the kitchen and steam lifts endlessly off the brown meniscus. Condensation on the cold window weeps. While Nick has lunch, my mother sips, puts her chin in her hands, and hangs out her eyes to dry in the insubstantial sunlight.

Not too soon. I'm sick of damp stains across my walls. Basement ruined. Tide ran as high as my toes, my knees, my thighs. Cold seepage through the mesh of my ribs. This Gerbil's thinking dry thoughts. I've done fish. I've done frog. I've had enough of water already. I'd like to tell her: Hey, my mother, you know the drill as well as I. You know what the baby books say about maternal stress and fetal development. Well, I'm telling you, my environment isn't exactly optimal. In fact, any more salt water and who can say how I'll come out? Back to the webbed toes I've so recently lost. Unabsorbed gills. Swollen arms like water wings. Or a swimsuit shaped birthmark? You want a baby or a starfish? How about a dolphin-daughter who slips like a silver tear from between your splayed legs? Think of that: a baby who squeaks in the night for tuna chunks. Add that to your list of monsters, my Gerbil mother.

But this woman, my mother, Maeve, sits perfectly still. To my tongue, uterine fluid tastes like sugar water, and she herself has something of the same unpleasant sweetness. Resignation, I guess. I'm not the first to make the claim; it's not the sort of comment to weigh on my conscience.

Ø

The empty days get emptier. The sun slips down the sky like, like — what should I say? — like a fried egg on a pane of glass? Too greasy? I dunno. I'm looking for a more playful sort of language, trying to keep up this exhausting narration — not good for a body, y'know, all this chatter. I'm a Gerbil not a squirrel. However the sun slips down the sky, my Gerbil mother gets up and crosses to the window to see how her first day alone again disappears into night. Outside, the evening sky still holds bright patches that might be the product of her tired eyes, or might be reflections in the window. Or might be ghosts. Mahon and Duncan, toking on the fire escape, disappearing in a puff of blue smoke. Other things ghost past too — silver flashes along drooping wires, along rungs of the iron fire escape, the last light of the day. My mother ghosts between the window and the stack of the washer–dryer. She leans back against the unit, bangs skull-plate to metal-skin. The washer–dryer sways, causing a full box of Zero to fall flat on the dryer's top. Soap flakes spill across the enamelled surface, and a few, loose flakes of soap waft upwards, drift down over my mother's head, fall between her and the window. She doesn't move. Standing by the darkening glass in the twilit room, she finds herself held fast by her own tired eyes. She's caught, transfixed by those last, lingering bright spots in the sky that might be something, might be nothing at all.

At long last, she puts out her hand, finds what she's looking for, presses up; the light drills down, a yellow incandescence. The window becomes a mirror. My mother finds herself looking into darkness, switches focus to her own tired face, to the dark rings under the nothings of her eyes. Outside, beyond the silvered window, the St. Clair streetcar rumbles by. She could ride it if she really wanted. What ties her to this suite of rooms is of her own choosing, she said so herself — a suit of rooms cut to measure. Go on, Mom, put on different clothes. Lace up your hip waders. Jam on your best straw boater. Find the door. Take your place in the world, the outside that belongs to all of us. Go down to the movies, my mother. To the clubs. To the parties that everyone else enjoys always. Or ... throw one yourself. Make complex, interior changes to your body, this apartment. Open-heart surgery. DIY organ transplant. Start small: find a CD, punch up some music. Lower the lights, and, if you won't exit through the door, at least open it to others. Let them in — the partiers, the holiday-makers, the good-time Charlies. Mahon wants you happy. My father wants you happy. The love of your life wants you happy. Least you can do is be happy.

And my mother begins to cry again.

Ø

A list of the things my mother does when left alone: wash the dishes that Mahon didn't do when he left; throw out the pasta pot (irredeemably burnt) that Mahon let boil dry; pick up the mess (discarded socks, shirts, pants) that Mahon left behind when packing; scrub the wall that Nick decorated with washable (who's kidding whom?) marker while his mother was busy cleaning up other messes; remove the marbles from the dryer (purpose unknown); mop up the juice under the table (discovered just as she finally sat to eat something); retrieve two day's worth of mail (junk and bills, what else?); despair over a crack in the front room window (when? how? who?); cry over the toys that Nick helped put away (tune: the Tidy-up song); cry while making her bed (round wet spots on the sheets like raindrops on the sidewalk); cry over nothing, nothing at all (it is over something, she tells herself — it *is*). Cry. Cry. Cry.

Ø

One day (but which?) a knock on the front door dries her tears, straightens her spine, widens her eyes. Who could it be? I feel a narrator's satisfaction at the appearance of a well-timed plot point but can claim no agency here — sometimes a Gerbil just gets lucky. Maeve wipes her teary cheeks with her sleeve, glances at her own fright-face in the mirror and decides not to bother to answer the door. Jeez.

Another knock. My mother-in-the-mirror grimaces. Waits. Two hearts tick, sometimes together, sometimes syncopated, never steady. Another knock. My mother has a thought, watches her own face turn anxious wondering: could it be him? Has he done it again and stolen back to her? Has he missed her that much? She runs, not walks, to the door.

At the door, Maeve remembers that Mahon has a key, wouldn't be knocking. My heart ticks on, steady and dependable, while hers stops, restarts only reluctantly. She sags against the wall, de-boned by disappointment.

Another knock. My mother screws up a minute share of curiosity, courage, one eye — in that order — and presses the other eye to the peephole. She examines the stranger who's been knocking at her door. The face in the hall is unnaturally circular, beach-balled by the lens. The peach disk swells, births a fist poised to knock again. My mother leans on tiptoes, feels the rat-a-tat-tat against her door-pressed belly — a steady rhythm like a second second heart. Through the peephole, the face dips, drops. My mother sees a forehead. A part in darkish hair. The wall. Then the face again, further away this time, disproportionately distant. A pale disk. Coming closer. Barrettes flash silver in the gloomy light of the landing — bars of argent, heraldic against hair as short and plush as fur.

The face comes from across the hall — the neighbour's face. No doubt about that. With the visionary clarity of the peephole, my mother can see that the door beyond the face stands open. Through the door, she sees purpled walls, window light slanting, yellow floorboards, everything fish-eyed. She can hear music, but faintly.

On the other side of the door, the face — the girl — takes a giant step backward, hands on knees, almost crouching, looking up into the peephole. Head to one side, she considers my mother's door. Then she straightens, stands arms akimbo, smiling at the door, smiling through the door. Green eyes, vivid in the half-light, unnerve my mother. Dream eyes. My mother wonders if she's awake.

I say: You're awake. Open the door, mother dearest. D'you hear me? D'you feel me pressing with my little hands? I'm sketching a door with my fingers, miming the knob, the weight in my fist. I'm eager for some diversion. I need a change from all the crying. D'you hear me, mother? Open the door.

Knock-knock.

Who's there?

Boo.

Boo Who?

Boo Hoo? Ha. Stop crying, Ma. Wipe your eyes. Wipe your nose. Answer the door.

But the door is already open.

The neighbour comes quickly forward on bare feet. Long eyes look us up and down. — Aw-w-w, she drawls, pauses on our threshold. The neighbour moves her hands to sketch something in the air. — Aw, look at you.

— Pardon? says my mother.

— Hey, says the neighbour, and she draws in the air again, round and wide. The gesture ends open-palmed, as if to say *there you are*. Or *we come in peace*. — Can I? says the neighbour turning over her hands and stretching them out toward us. — You don't mind. (Not a question.) She advances. The tips of her nails sparkle; she wears rings on her fingers, rings on her toes. But the toes hardly register. The fingers are what alarm me, reaching toward my mother, toward Gerbil. Reaching. Reaching. Touching. My mother ought to step back. But.

—What? says my dumb mother.

Too late. Contact. The fingers brush against the cotton of my mother's T-shirt and settle lightly. Eight fingertips spread in two rows on either side of her inconspicuous belly. Hardly a touch. Barely contact. But a little electric shock.

My mother jumps. I jump.

Ø

The two women wait in the kitchen for the kettle to boil. My mother takes deep breaths, keeps looking sideways at the neighbour whose name turns out to be Darcy. Darcy grins back. She looks prepared for Maeve smarten up, to shake off her lethargy, to focus clearly on Darcy's self with all the attention she so richly deserves. C'mon, the grin seems to say, there's something I need. The grin embarrasses my mother so much that she opens, closes her mouth. Back in the hallway, that grin caused my mother to flap her hands intending to urge Darcy out but somehow urging her in. Now she finds herself fussing over cups and teaspoons. The kettle boils and my mother plays Mother: she pours the tea, passes milk, passes sugar.

—These walls, y'know, says Darcy, having settled herself with her cup. She knocks on the communicating wall between her apartment and ours. —Thin. Not much of a sound barrier. Not at all.

My mother considers the music she's heard drifting through that wall, laughter. Does she consider her own sobbing, her moaning, her whining a fair exchange for some subpar pop music, a dance hit or two? I'm sure I don't know. Neither, it appears, does my mother. She doesn't know where to look. Won't look at Darcy's teasing smile, looks instead for Nick, who hides, lurking bright-eyed around the door frame of his room. From the moment Darcy entered our apartment, Nick has been stricken with an inexplicable shyness. My mother's shyness is no more explicable but even more hateful to her — a heavy old coat that constricts. Maeve looks hard at Nick, beckons to him, shakes her head when he sinks back further into the shadows. My mother would spare him shyness if she could. She would. She would do anything to stop him from turning into her. Who wouldn't?

Darcy's been watching the two of them, moving her eyes from my mother to Nicholas and back again. — Cute little guy, says Darcy, looking down at the table when my mother looks her way. Darcy eyes the sugar bowl instead, tips sugar straight from the bowl into her mug. She stirs vigorously with her teaspoon then sucks it. — Sweet, she says indistinctly, her mouth flashing silver. Her spoon goes into her mouth, comes out with a loud pop.

— Sweet? says my mother, alarmed by the pop. — Nick?

Darcy laughs at my mother's confusion. — Sure, she says. — He's sweet. Sugar's sweet. You're the sweetest of all. Look at you, look how sweet. Darcy takes her own advice, this time looks hard at my mother. A serious once-over. A scrutinizing stare. X-ray specs. My mother moves ever so slightly, as if to cover herself — a hand curled over top and bottom. But by now Darcy has finished her inspection, brief as it was intense. She's checking out the kitchen instead, taking in the cupboards, the sink, the refrigerator and the microwave. The dirty fingerprints. The unwashed laundry. One of Nick's greyest blandscapes — unmitigated gloom. Maeve thinks she can guess what's in this stranger's mind, can sense the critical assessment, the harsh judgment, the rejection.

— Your apartment's just like mine, Darcy tells my mother.

— I doubt that, says my mother, in a voice that's as grey and unhappy as Nick's artwork.

— Sure. Just the same. Only backward. Darcy thinks over what she's just said, laughs. — A mirror image. One of us must be Alice.

My mother opens, closes her mouth.

— You know ... in Wonderland.

My mother doesn't get Alice. She doesn't see Wonderland. She sees a strange girl in her kitchen, a girl with a perfectly flat, smooth stomach under her crop top. My mother can see Darcy's belly button, an outie like a flipped eyelid. Every part of Darcy watches my mother. My mother swivels in her chair, avoids scrutiny. She feels this stranger's gaze scraping her to the bone. My mother sniffs. Just nerves, but still she sniffs and wipes a tear from her leaky eyes.

— Oh my, says Darcy. — What's the trouble?

— No trouble.

— Go on. Tell Auntie Darcy. Boyfriend trouble?

— Husband, my mother corrects, out of habit.

— Get out, says Darcy. She squirms in her chair, like she's never heard anything so extraordinary in her whole life. — Get out. Married? For what — for how long?

— Five years.

— And the kid? He's what — how old?

— Almost three.

Darcy does the math. Truly. My mother watches. One. Two. — Get out, says Darcy again, more mildly this time, bored by the respectability of the sum. — Well, you look great, she adds. — I mean, other than the red eyes and stuff. And your nose.

My mother tries to speak, should say something, can't find anything to say.

— Is the tea okay? You want more?

— I hate tea, says Darcy. My mother blinks and Darcy laughs. — Just being nosy. Just getting myself through the door. Serves me right.

My mother jumps to her feet, flings open a cupboard door, rockets to the fridge, pulls on the silver handle. — Oh no, she says. Oh no. I've got ...

— Don't, says Darcy.

— Juice.

— No, really. Don't. Stop. Sit down.

My mother drops back into her chair. She lifts her mug in her hands, hides behind the rising steam, holds her hands in front of her face. Tries to gather wits, shards of pride. Straightens her back, giving me some much needed space. Deep breath for both of us.

— I'm sorry, says my mother, if we've been disturbing you. Through the thin walls and everything.

— Oh, don't worry about that. I don't like quiet.

My mother, whose life's ambition is a little peace and quiet, succumbs to mild astonishment.

— I like noise. Makes me feel at home. I like your kid — Noah?

— Nick.

— Nick. He's nice and noisy. Like a little brother, only always in another room. Which is good. Best really.

— How old are you? asks my mother, who seems to have fallen under some kind of compulsion and can't help herself. She hears herself, trails off, losing nerve in a big way.

Darcy ignores the question, puts her teaspoon back in the sugar. Stirs. — No, I like knowing that someone's home next door, hearing you move around. It's a good feeling really: knowing you're not alone. Don't you think?

— I guess so, says my mother, who has obviously never thought about noise this way. She puts her hand on my roof, as if to check on her other neighbour, as if the thought of someone moving nearby brings me to mind. I lie still. Won't give her the satisfaction. — I guess it's a kind of comfort, she says doubtfully.

— Sure it is, says Darcy. — When you're all alone.

— All alone, echoes my mother mournfully. What a drama queen.

Darcy paddles with her teaspoon in the sugar bowl, absorbed in the gentle swishing sound she's making. 'Round and 'round goes her spoon. — Where's Mahon now? she asks, keeping her spoon moving.

— Mahon? For a millisecond Maeve had stopped thinking about him, had her mind on other things.

Darcy stirs the sugar more vigorously, lifts some out, lets it fall back into the bowl like a rain of crystal teardrops. She lifts her green eyes, meeting Maeve's red and bloodshot ones. As for me, for Gerbil, I've got my eyes screwed closed. I'm slapping my forehead with my palm. I'm like, Hey Mom. Earth to Mom. Heads up, Mama. Didn't ya hear what she said?

— Mahon? Oh, he's gone again. They play Thursday to Sunday. Monday's a drive day, Tuesday I dunno, then Wednesday and ... oh, I don't remember. I've got a schedule. Oh.

Hear that sound? That's me — more head-slapping. Ladies and gentlemen, my mother. My idiot mother. She missed it, she missed it. Can you believe? She missed. It.

— Where did I put the schedule?

Darcy lifts her eyebrows, then takes her teaspoon from the sugar bowl and sticks it in her mouth again. Darcy is not sweet. Not in the least. Ohmygod, she's *not* sweet.

My mother is crying again. Turns out she can't remember where she left the schedule. — And the phone number too, she tells Darcy. — There's a cell number on the back. What if I need it? I might need it.

— You think something could go wrong?

— No. No, everything will be fine.

— Then you're crying because everything will be all right.

— No — well, yes. No.

My thick mother. My dense mother. My water-logged and sodden mother. I'd like to finish the drowning she started, my tear-stained Gerbil mother. I'd like to push her head down into herself and hold. No mercy. None. Hold until the bubbles stop: that would be my motto. Submerge until the surface of her was calm and still. Leave her, like Ophelia, white-faced and newly aquatic under the ripples. No mercy. That's what I'd do to my mother — don't get me started on that Mahon.

Darcy looks up. Sucks on her teaspoon. Grins.

Ø

But if I were Maeve, this is what I would do. I would wear a little shirt like this Darcy does — I could if I really wanted to. And low-rise jeans too. Show a chunk of flesh — red and streaky. Connect up stretch marks with a tattooed web, each scar a different strand. And in the middle, a navel ring shaped like a spider. That's what I would do.

But my mother only places a hand on her well-covered belly.

— Gonna pop? says Darcy, between licks of her teaspoon.

— Always possible, says my mother, distracted. — And don't do that to the sugar.

Ø

The day unravels. Darcy takes my mother into the living room, causes her to put away train tracks and plush toys until the floor appears. Then, she finds Nick's books on their shelf by the window, pulls down a couple, curls up on some cushions. My mother forcibly removes Nick from hiding, places him in her lap for a mother–son cameo. Nick is not content. What does he know, my brother?

Darcy holds out one of Nick's picture books. — I like this one, she says. She shows the picture to my mother, traces a scudding mark from left to right. My mother sits up straighter, looks at Darcy with new attention. Darcy continues to flip through the pages, stopping now and again to look closely at the drawings, sometimes to put her finger on the glossy paper. Overleaf, Darcy settles her palm flat on a broad area of colour.

— You like that one, asks my mother. Darcy nods.

Yes, thinks my mother. Of course. Yes.

Darcy picks up another book and opens it. — Oooh, she says, and turns the page. Then she's quiet for a long, long time, turning pages. Looking.

Maeve leans back and closes her eyes. Blots of watercolour

pigment pool and dry behind tired lids. A wash of gouache subsides more gently, opaquely staining the whiteness. Colours blend, swirl, slow, then dry to palest shades: mauve, rose, winter sunshine. Black greys, then silvers. Blue cools, then greys. Tears fall, vanish magically into paper, leave behind only the slightest quaver in the fibre. Underneath, a hairline crack, a tiny fault, a pencil mark from here to here.

— Mommy!

My mother opens her eyes. Nick has grown bored of being shy, stares at Darcy with unreserved animosity. — Yes, Nick?

— Mommy?

— Yes, Nick?

— Mommy?

The same, old joke.

— What do you want, Nicholas?

— I want da book, Mommy.

I say: Excellent Nick. Commendable my brother. Fight the good fight.

Maeve reaches down, hands him a book from the stack at her feet.

— No, Mommy, Nick says gravely, I want dat book. He points at Darcy, makes himself crystal clear. Leaves no room for error.

— Here, Nick. You can have *this* book, says my mother in a reasonable tone of voice. — Darcy is reading that book right now.

— Uh-uh. You give me dat book. He points again. My good brother, so certain, so expressive in his speech, and with such a restricted lexical range. Bodes well.

My mother shakes her head. — No, Nick. I will give you dat book — *that* book — when Darcy is done.

Oooh. That word: the 'no' word. I expect a blow-up, a small, child-celled, thermonuclear explosion, but I am disappointed. Nick takes 'no' in stride. He looks at his mother through half-closed eyes: a long, evaluating look. — Daddy gives me cookies, Nick says at last, unexpectedly.

My mother's brow wrinkles audibly, at least for me, located

down here next to her soul. — Cookies? she says, frowning again. *Cookies?*

Nick snorts and sniffs, working up to something big. — I love cookies, Mommy, he says with maximum intensity. Then the kicker. — I love Daddy.

Well, that takes our collective breath away: Nick playing both sides against the middle. Divide and conquer: Nick's new motto. Well done, my brother. Very tricksy. If only your plan could work; if only it weren't so painfully — that's *ouchy* to you, Nick — obvious. Look now, our mother already begins to laugh. She sees right though you, Saint Nicholas.

But I'm wrong. Or rather, I'm too right — clever Gerbil. Nick-in-the-lap gets a little hug from his mommy. She's amused by his stratagem, his ruse, his ploy. This Maeve, this mother, laughs, and a spark of contentment takes to the air butterfly-wise, launching itself somewhere between her sternum and my picture window. We both sense it take flight, fluttery and indigestible. When I see it swoop by, I reach for my fly swatter.

— Do *you* want a cookie, Nick? says my mother, in a wheedling tone of voice. — Is that what you want? Funny old Nicky — isn't he funny.

No.

— Do *you* want a cookie, Nicky? Should we share with Darcy?

Nick won't commit. Thinks his position too strong. Imagines he's scored big, knows the smart money plays things cool when holding the cards. Card sharp Nick. Poker-faced Nick and his self-deluding mother, now known as The Rube. The sucker. The mark. She dumps Nick on the chesterfield in her hurry to bring back a plate of cookies, to offer the plate around.

— Nick? Just one, sweetheart. Just — okay, two. Only two, honey. No, Nick. Oh no. No, leave that one, Darcy, you don't have to take it. No, don't give it back to him; no, don't give — well, just three, Nick. Three cookies only, and that's final. That's all. Pass me the plate, Darcy. Give it here. Watch out for — oh, never mind.

∅

— You draw? my mother asks a while later. The cookie plate sits empty. Nick lies across her knees, eating the last cookie and swinging his legs. She puts up a hand to keep his feet from hitting her in her crumb-covered face.

Darcy looks up from the picture book and considers the question. — Good work is always easy to recognize, says Darcy, which is no kind of answer but seems to satisfy my mother. — I like this, Darcy says, and she begins to read in a sing-song voice: — Once upon a time ...

— Just a second, says my mother, who wriggles on the chesterfield, trying to find a more convenient location for my house, for the Gerbil dome. I am rocked to and fro, but don't thank her. My living room receives an extension, but I lose a spare room. What was I keeping in there? — God, says my mother. — I can hardly breathe.

— Ready now? asks Darcy, and, finding my mother settled with Nick in what's left of her lap, she begins to read. — Once upon a time, there lived a woodsman and his wife who could never agree on which of them worked harder. One day, after a particularly long argument ...

— I know this one, interrupts Maeve.

— ... the woodsman and his wife decided to switch jobs.

— Oh, please, says Maeve.

— The wife went off in the morning and walked long and far into the forest. When she reached its blackest depths, she took out her axe and began to chop. The woodsman stayed home, imagining that he would begin his day by sleeping late.

— Ha, says my mother, and settles down to listen.

— No sooner had he closed his eyes than the baby began to cry.

— Of course, says my mother.

Darcy stops reading and holds up the book so that Maeve can see the picture. A nest of squiggly ink marks forms the woodsman's face, while an elegant round of the pen separates baby's head from virgin paper. My mother and Darcy nod knowingly.

Ø

Darcy says she has to go. I can't see the back of her fast enough. My head hurts. A Gerbil needs time to think, to be alone. My mother, on the other paw, expresses dissatisfaction at Darcy's intention to depart, urges her to stay a little longer. What does she think she's playing at, my mother? How can she be so stupid.

Darcy won't be persuaded, but she has something for my mother. Something she'd like her to see. My mother claps her hands together, Nick mimicking her from the chesterfield where he stands. Clap. Bounce.

— Some of your work? trills my mother. — I'd love to see it.

Ad'd luv to seeeee it. God, I hate her.

Darcy nods modestly, heads across the hall to her own apartment. Both doors stand open. Yellow light spills from one into the other, mixes it up. Very friendly. Neighbourly like. Shucks.

In Darcy's absence, my mother takes up the picture book she'd been reading. She flips through the pages, gazing again at careful drawings of catastrophe. In one, the cow grazes on a tufted roof of pen marks. In the next, curving scratches etch a rope that connects cow via chimney to the woodsman's ankle. In the next picture, porridge boils over in a torrent of inky bubbles. My mother turns to the last page, to the upward strokes of the woodsman's face as he reunites with his wife, kisses his wife, joins his graphic energy to hers. My mother looks at this page for a long time, even touches the page with her finger. But she doesn't cry. Miraculously, her fluid gauges empty. Her tear tank dry. My mother's got nothing left — I wish I could be glad.

And then Darcy's back with something in her hand. Darcy, who used to be bold and dumb, has turned shy and smart. Some kind of transformation, like a werewolf maybe? In her hand is a sheaf of papers — really a set of thin, paper-bound booklets —

which she gives to my mother. Then she ducks across the hall, disappears behind her own door.

My mother takes the books back inside, looks at the topmost cover. Darcy's face, rendered in squiggles and curves, stares back. Overtop sits the title in decorated block letters, and underneath, in a tiny, timid lowercase, is Darcy's name. My mother smiles to herself. Yes, smiles. Folds back the cover.

The telephone is ringing.

Ø

Seconds pass. Blood rushes in, rushes out. Nerves fire. Messages shoot brain-ward. In my mother's apartment, the telephone still rings. An alarm bell sounds in my house too. What kind of a bell? One of those doorbells embellished with a pair of gilt half notes? A handbell, the kind used by a schoolteacher in a one-room school? A three bell? A nine bell? A twenty-one bell salute?

Nick reaches the phone first, lays his hand on the receiver, knows this is forbidden and turns a pair of wall-eyes on our Mother. Maeve picks up the phone.

— 'Lo.

A prim voice informs her that she has a collect call from a David Mahon. Will she accept the charges? Yes, she will, and so fast I have no time to kick her, to pummel her, to break her ribs. They have to talk; there are things I want to know.

— Yes, yes.

— Maeve!? Our father. Yelling. The noise behind him hurts our ears. Drowns out all familiarity. Human qualities of timbre and tone. Of decency and distinction. Or were those lost some other way? Either way, my mother rabbits on.

— Mahon? Is that you?

(Duh.)

— It's me. It's me.

— I can hardly hear you.

— What?

— I can't hear you!

— Just a minute. I can't hear you.

(Why do they carry on like a bad Vaudeville act?)

— Is this quieter? My father still shouts — the noise around him downgraded but hardly harmless.

— A little, says my mother.

— I wanted to call before you went to bed.

— Not yet.

— What's that?!

— Not yet. We're not in bed yet.

— The guys are tuning. Sound check.

— Sounds like it.

— Sounds like what?!

— Sounds loud.

— Oh yeah. Ha. It's loud all right.

(Idiot. Sorry — *idiots*.)

— Maeve?

— I'm still here.

— I was sitting at the bar, y'know, waiting. And I saw this phone and I thought, Mahon, you've been thinking about them all day — now is your chance to call.

— You're calling from the bar? Good thinking, Mahon.

(I'm struck by one thing — *Gerbil* is struck by one thing. My mother, I'm starting to wonder if bits of her exist that ... I mean, he's got some explaining to do, and she's asking all the wrong questions, but still she seems ... Nah.)

— It *was* good thinking. Don't know if I'd have time to call later.

— So much to do.

— What?

— So much to — never mind. Did you have a good day?

— 's all right. Sleeping mostly.

— ...

— You?

— No, Mahon. I never sleep. It's one of my little problems.

— What? Missed most of that.

— Actually, I did.

— What?

— I did. I did have a good day.

— Good.

— I met ...

— Listen Maeve. Dave's waving. I think ...

(Muffled shouting. The sound of band noise absorbed by shirt and skin — we're held tight to his chest while he negotiates. We sigh in tandem. I hate the fact, but we do. We sigh as one, single happy-unhappy creature. One thought. His shirt. His skin.)

— Maeve?!

(Why does he never call me by name?)

— Maeve? Are you there?

— Where would I go?

— Huh? Love to Nick. He good?

— He's good.

(Me. Me. I'm better.)

— Okay then. This isn't so bad.

— ...

— Maeve, I have to go now.

— ...

— My time is up. I'll call again tomorrow.

— We can't really afford these calls, Mahon. You don't have to ...

— What?!

— Don't ...

— No, I have to go, Maeve. Tell me tomorrow.

My mother sighs. Heavily.

— Good night, Maeve.

— Good night, Mahon.

(Good night, you bastard.)

Ø

My problems come bubbling back up from the basement drain. They discolour the rugs. They disfigure the walls. They leave a black, inky stain all over my house.

I have no way of stopping her, of warning her, so my mother takes Darcy's books to bed with her — her real bed this time, not a makeshift dog-bed under the dining room table. She's back in the real bed. No more floating face down — no more drowning — in her misery. And I'm not complaining, understand. I'm not sorry she's managed to drain her damp humours. Wrung herself out. Stretched herself to dry. I'm not upset and I'm certainly not worried. Gerbils never worry — it's not what we do. We never shiver and shake. All the same, just this once, I'd like to have a word in her ear. I'd like to counsel her, as she props herself up on her side of the bed, laying Darcy's comics (that's what the books are) on her knees. Nothing specific, understand, just a, well, a non-specific caution. Something like, watch yourself, my mother. You've got Jell-O under your feet now, tremulous and shaky as the flab of my roof, of your belly. Just watch yourself, Maeve. Just pay attention.

Maeve minutely examines the cover of issue one. She gently turns back the page, taking care not to crease the cover, and right from page one she likes what she sees. The mess in Darcy's Wonderland makes her smile. The fridge sits bare but the counters are covered, are stacked with dishes and pots and dirty spoons. Familiar, huh? Sure. There's Darcy! My mother reads, looks closer. Turns a page. Reads. Turns another. Converts ink to sense and back again. Darcy on every page: ink to action, action to ink. Oh, who cares? So Darcy can draw. Look instead at Darcy and the things she does: the sequence that ends in the bedroom, the sequence that ends in the dirty joke, ends in a blush, ends in an argument, ends in the hallway outside our place. Maeve, look at our door, drawn freehand. I'm holding my Gerbil breath. Where am I, then, I wonder — where are we? Where's my father? Behind that paper square, sitting, waiting on the far side of nothing? Darcy draws our stairwell, our front entrance with the mailboxes. And wait. Whose tail is that disappearing around the corner? I get no answer. My mother couldn't care less, only breathes deeper, pleased to be out of her own head for a while. I can hardly look. Cover my bright eyes with my paws.

My mother reads on.

Darcy's stories, half in words and half in lines, keep my mother propped up in bed late into the night. She reads the first two books, closing each even as she reaches for the next. I want her to stop; I want to sleep. She keeps me up. I listen to the overhead ratcheting of her breathing as I fold back my covers, kick off my slippers, say my prayers. Scrape. Scrape. I lie awake, listening. I've forgotten how to find forgetfulness.

The last story of the last book takes up only a few pages. My mother begins to read eagerly. I glance up and can't help but notice that this time Darcy has drawn the milk store across the street with its counter full of lottery tickets and the mounted television that's always on. Sometimes my mother stands transfixed by a bit of Bollywood broadcast to the store at large. Then the woman at the counter has to recall my mother to herself, summon back her soul from an Indian sound stage where she doesn't dance and doesn't sing — not my mother, remember? Darcy draws this woman behind the counter most carefully, indicating the fall of her sari, the lightness of her eyes. Darcy draws herself slipping a can of tomatoes into her coat. She's a terrible person, Darcy, and we look her full in the face — a frame dedicated to looking at Darcy watching the woman behind the counter. Over the page the woman behind the counter has been distracted by a customer. I recognize the customer. My mother. Nick in the stroller. We're in Darcy's comic. Reduced to lines, we're in the frame.

In real life, my mother sucks air.

In the frame, my mother reverses the process, expels air, produces a speech bubble: *a book of bus tickets,* says my mother-in-the-comic.

In the next frame, I see the same picture but a new bubble, although this one doesn't seem to come from my mother's mouth. This speech bubble hovers oddly in the middle of the frame and says this: *And a pack of Export As, please.*

The shop woman has her back to my mother now, getting something from the shelf behind her. Darcy's pen picks out my mother in profile, and you can tell she's transfixed by the television. In the background of the cartoon, Darcy shoves a squarish package of dehydrated soup into her coat.

Two smallish frames, one after the other. My mother says, *What's this?* She holds up the cigarettes. The shop woman says, *What you asked for.*

Penultimate frame, slightly larger. *I don't want these,* says my mother. Darcy's drawn her face-on, with her coat open. You can see the bulge of me spreading the zippered edges, distending her shirt.

Last frame: my mother from the side, preceded by stroller and belly bulge. Now the speech bubble clearly comes from her midsection, says: *Ain't I a stinker.*

It's me. It's Gerbil. Seen. Caught. I look at the ink Darcy on the page. She's in the background with her coat full, shrugging, making me afraid.

How did she know?

In bed, in real life, my mother smiles. Re-examines her tiny paper doppelgänger at some length. Reads the comic again and again. Breathes through her nose. Stares at a spot on the wall and, for once, I can't guess what she's thinking. I'm shaking and scared, too rattled to know. Now she closes the comic. Now she turns off the light. Now she closes her eyes. Goes to sleep.

Goes to sleep. Just like that.

And this time it's me, Gerbil, who lies awake. Can't get comfortable. My four-poster seems bigger than ever, the duvet a spreading glacier, and I feel cold the second I slip between the sheets. Soon I crawl out again, pull on a dressing gown, thick and soft as a boa constrictor's gullet. I stagger about in fancy cat's paw slippers, more gripped than shod, until I shrug off such dangerous finery and stand in my own thin pelt, shivering. Hardly so much as a square of moonlight enters my bedchamber. Not much light to wonder by. And to wonder about what? About dark and light, about pen and ink? That joker, Darcy? Me and Mahon behind our walls of archival quality illustration board? I don't get it, or maybe I do — I just don't like it. I curl up on the floor of my room, but still I can't sleep. I get up, pace the floorboards, listening to the scritch, the scratch, of my own toenails. I wander through shadowy rooms, each delineated by nothing more than a single, curved line stretching up, disappearing into the dark. Examined more closely, these lines, which appear thick and firmly drawn, dissolve into tiny dots, into halftones. The panels of the hallway disintegrate into cross-hatching, leaving me nowhere safe to stand, to lean, until inky shadows spread. Blot. Run like tears.

I GET THROUGH THE NIGHT LISTENING TO HEARTBEATS: me, her, me, her, me, her. I doze a little, but in the morning I'm still exhausted. By the rosy light of dawn, my cottage sprouts red roses on the wallpaper, red armchair on the rug, red fire in the grate, but I'm not tempted to get up, to get out of bed. I pull the bedcovers over my head. I, Gerbil, hide.

's not right.

∅

My mother wakes to the telephone ringing, expects Mahon, gets a bright, professional voice. Could Maeve ever sound like that?

— Mrs. Mahon? Mavis?

— Not Mavis.

— I'm sorry, ma'am. Is she there? May I speak with her?

— I'm her. I'm not Mavis.

The bright, professional voice has no practice with my mother's telephone style, not experienced, as is my father, in the loops and dead ends of her conversation. The voice falls silent, obviously trying to work with the unmatched puzzle pieces of sense my mother produces as an inevitable by-product of existing. A moment later, the voice gives up, starts at the beginning again. Good choice, voice.

— Good morning. Mrs. Mahon, I'm calling with a friendly reminder. Your scheduled doctor's appointment approaches.

— Approaches?

An editorial qualification, on my mother's part — a minor quibble with word choice. With diction. This time the professional voice won't be sucked in, won't be baffled.

— Approaches, she says, firmly, and she spiels off a time and a date. My mother sighs, knows she's recorded this appointment on her calendar. — I'll be there, says Maeve. Says my mother, and hangs up.

chapter seven

We roll over, look out the bedroom window. Looks warmer, outside. How long have we been sleeping? Has spring come? Have the snows gone, turned to meltwater, and thrown themselves on the black bones of the ridged soil? Is St. Clair covered in daffodils? Cars stopped, parked higgledy-piggledy, abandoned on a carpet of sudden yellow? Are the bees buzzing? Swarms of bees. Flocks of bees. Hoards of bees. Armies of bees. Loud enough (at least) to fill the apartment. Loud enough to —

— I hear you, Nick.

My mother gets up — eyes bag, breasts droop. She balances herself vertically; the rest of her sorts itself on a horizontal axis. This bit here. This bit there. Nick stands upright in his crib, buzzing, his lips in a wet blur. As soon as he sees her, he stops, cries.
— I a airplane, Mommy. A airplane.

— Excellent, Nick, says my mother. — Saves me a lot of work: changing, feeding, entertaining you. Shall I just open the window for you? Fly away?

— Yep, Mommy. Yep.

Maeve goes to the window. The ghostly image of Mahon in his running hat superimposes itself over the grey street below. A moment later, he's gone. A haunted apartment this. Very haunted.

— Upsy-Daisy. Maeve lifts Nick out of his crib, and, in the same movement, out of his diaper. The diaper, soaked and loosened by little hands, plops back onto the sheet. A little poop rolls out, a tiny turd. It lies there, inches away from Nick's comforter. Nobody says a word. We all stare.

— Poopy, says Nick at last. Thoughtfully. Reflectively.

— Yes, Nick. You might have warned me.

— Poopy, says Nick. (He's warning her now.)

— I airplane, says Nick.

— Buzzzzz, says Nick.

My mother says nothing. Best she can do.

Ø

My mother knocks on Darcy's door. No one answers. She has the comics in one hand, a smile on her face. A thank you in her heart — I feel it lodged in there. A giant card with a funny (ha ha) caption and a signature in ink. Hearts and bloody flowers.

No one answers and my mother turns around. Crosses the hallway. Goes home.

Ø

My mother's been reading again. Not Darcy's books — not them. She's been scanning her collection of baby books, that claque of tongue-wagging paper faces advising her, warning her, alarming her. Village woman with leathery skins, broken teeth, crooked fingers. Crouched in the middle of my mother's living room, the old bags shake their heads and croak on and on. They never agree, those dried-up witches; they offer no comfort. No comfort either from the ones that come later, the lab-coated, clip boarded alchemists of motherhood — changing it into this, into that, into something socio-cultural, into something natural, into nothing achievable. Scanning those baby books with eyes stretched wide, my mother sits, sated but hardly satisfied, on the chesterfield. She stares at the video she's put in for Nick (electronic babysitter, sneer the old hags, the learned doctors — where the hell are they when she needs a flesh and blood helper?). My mother stares but doesn't see. She tunes out the cartoon spirits, sprites, imps of distress and disaster flitting across the screen. Inky creatures, half human, half animal. Smart remarks. Sketchy expressions. What might they tell her, all these marks on the screen? What can they tell me, Gerbil? I shut my eyes, but Maeve won't shut hers. Won't close her lids. Mom? C'mon, Mother. Shut 'em.

My mother wanders down to her bedroom, steps over Mahon's socks, still on the floor. From under the bed, she pulls a small suitcase. She unzips the suitcase, begins to pack: a clean nightgown

I've never seen before, a pair of slippers, a housecoat that's seen better days, a stack of her magazines. From the bathroom, she brings a toothbrush still cellophaned into its box, a brush, a comb, a small travel toothpaste. I'll admit. She has my attention now. What's this all about? A trip — are we going on a trip? Will she go running after Mahon? Would she really brave buses and blizzards to bring him home from the not-so-far north? Snatching her husband back from Dave's jaws. Dave's grinning maw.

She's packing strange things now. A disposable camera. A tennis ball in a length of nylon stocking (the whole thing unearthed from the back of a drawer). A bottle of baby oil (crusty-capped, likely leaky). Everything goes into the small suitcase. My mother closes the lid and looks around. I wait. I wait for her to pick up the suitcase, carry it into the front hall. Call a cab? Hail a taxi? Why not fly Air Nick into the heart of the storm?

My mother does none of these things. She zips up her suitcase and places it under the bed. Straightens painfully and crosses her arms. There. Finished. Over.

Oh, job well done, my mother. A good day's work. And I'm not asking, not even curious. I couldn't care less. Wouldn't dream of shouting, what's with the suitcase? Why is it under the bed? What are you up to, my mother? I won't ask and her lips are sealed. She's hardly even breathing. Hardly living. Only a shade of my mother, one more ghost joining Mahon and Duncan, insubstantial smoke on the fire escape. So many memories in this haunted apartment. My mother, Maeve, drifts back toward the living room, crosses her own spectral footprints — herself in memory gliding up and down once, twice, so many times. We leave ectoplasmic mess on the rug, so hard to clean, worse than poop-on-a-sheet. Too many grubby footprints. Nick's. My father's. Look closely and something else materializes: a vaporous Gerbil, pushed to and fro by time's tides. Bluish streaks of paws, tail-tip, ears. Dark flashes of eye-shine in the shadows, three feet off the ground. Months and months of me: a mist smeared hallway. Not my hallway. Not my house. Cover my eyes.

Lift my paws. My mother sits with Nick in front of the video. Nobody's saying a word.

Ø

They say you can't go home again. I can. My house never leaves me — a constant constant. I love my house as much as I hate — as I *dislike* — my mother. Two separate entities, my mother and my house. My mother has ribs, a bladder, a pelvis. My house has beams, a four-poster, a home theatre. See. Not the same. Not at *all the* same.

My library, now. A place I really adore. Long stretch of inlaid floor, arched windows on one side, and, in the pilastered alcoves on the other side, so many bookshelves. And such books. Faces and Backs. Spines. Books of flesh and blood, coming alive in your hands as you read them. Books lined with teeth. Gentle books that mumble at your fingers with a horse's velvet lips. Armoured books with bony plates, inside and out. Books staked on tables. Books left on chairs. Sitting. Speaking. Sliding. Walking on end with their pages hanging slackly in between the striding boards. My books. I'm reading now. Gerbil parses her collection. Such a collection. A body of work. Such secrets. I'm not saying a word.

Ø

— Nick? You want a sandwich for lunch? PB and jam?

— Yes, Mommy.

— Wash your hands then.

(A series of wandering scuffs and thuds.)

— Use the stool, Nicky. Let Mommy help.

(Running water. Splashing.)

— There.

Ø

The library disappoints. A big mess. Books everywhere. Who's been chucking stuff around? Who's responsible? Crazy feeling my mother's been in here. Been rooting though, looking for something. Crazy feeling.

No, she's out there — a moment's confusion. Watch her riffling through stacks of paper, lifting up old magazines, pawing through piles of books. Looking for something misplaced. — Where is it? She hisses. Sighs. Slaps her forehead. — Where did I leave it?

I head out to my terrace, accessible from the library through a huge (a *huge,* Maeve) set of French doors. But once outside, the weather proves flat and grey. The sea featureless. Even the palm trees seem flat. Gerbil turns her back on the dull weather, stretches out on her own deck chair overlooking the water. Wears a big, floppy hat, a string bikini (because I can). Gerbil can rub in her own suntan lotion. Pour her own drinks from the pitcher on the rattan table. Gerbil puts on her sunglasses and covers her eyes. Won't let anyone see her eyes. Tired. Red-rimmed. Dry.

Ø

— The weather should be changing, Maeve tells Nick. Afternoon stretches and both of them have been inside far too long. — An endless winter, says Maeve. — But almost spring. I can feel things changing. Do you, Nick? Do you feel things changing?

— Park, says Nick.

— No, says Maeve.

— Park, says Nick.

— No, says Maeve.

— Park, says Nick.

— All right, says Maeve. If you insist.

But Gerbil says, stay away from the cracks in the windows. Keep your head down low. Avoid drafts. Avoid doors, windows. Avoid the outside. But above all, avoid the park in winter.

Ø

The sidewalks are clear enough to use the stroller. Maeve pushes Nick down St. Clair. They have a couple of choices. A little park nearby: a climber, a fence with a gate, houses nearby to stare at (hoping to see someone emerge, do something interesting). Or. A big park some way away: slides, several climbers, old oak trees (bare now, but still elegant), a view down the hill toward downtown. Hmmm. Big park? Little park?

In the end, the cold breeze shooting up the street decides both for the little park. They are utterly unique in making that decision today; they are the only ones there. Stale footprints in snow suggest a well-used place, but today my mother and Nick have it to themselves.

Nick sports a purple snowsuit, blue mitts, a blue toque pulled down low over his eyes, hood pulled up over the toque. His boots are also purple, with a well-worn rabbit printed on each. Purple Nick heads for the climber, struggles to mount the ramp, his boots slipping on the icy wood. Poor Nick. His cheap boots transmogrify in the winter cold into flat skates, the plastic soles becoming slippery discs good only for sliding. Can't she afford something decent? (I know the answer — don't tell me.)

Nick slides. Adaptable, flexible Nick. He pulls himself up the ramp and slides down. Pulls himself up, slides down. Up, down. All the time, calling — Mommy, Mommy, see me. Lookit me.

My mother looks. Her eyes tear up at the touch of the frigid wind but still she looks.

— Good, Nick. Keep going.

— Mommy come.

But Mommy can't come. Her knees have frozen solid, locked in position. She's captured a bubble of warmish air in the collar of her coat. If she moves she'll leak that warmth away. She'll die.

— Mommy come.

— Nick, she groans. No, Nick.

Nick looks at her across the small park, not broad enough to hide the expression of disappointed hostility she sees in his eyes.

— Mommy's cold, she tries to explain, but Nick doesn't *do* other people's feelings. Maeve's gone to the park in winter. With a psychopath.

A new game: jumping off the climber. Maeve knows this game. Jumping off the climber: number one on the list of reasons to avoid not just this park, but all parks. The jumping scares her. Alarms her. Makes her sit up, pay attention. Lets cold atmosphere into her airlock.

— No, Nick, stop.

— I a airplane, Mommy.

— No, no, you're not Nick. Stop jumping. Please.

Now she has to get up. Now she has to abandon herself to the cutting wind that makes everything so much colder than necessary. Keep your head low, Maeve. Avoid the cold blow. Avoid the gaps in your coat. Above all, avoid the park in winter.

Nick jumps. Maeve stands beside the climber, orders him to stop. Nick picks his way up the slippery wooden rungs, reaches the top and jumps again.

— Nick. No. If only, she thinks, just for a second, he'd actually fall, and hurt himself — then we could all go home. Maeve's already sorry, bites her lip. Like the wicked Queen, she draws blood. Does this make her evil too — our bad lady of the endless winter?

Nick jumps. Jumps again. Jumps.

— Don't, says my mother. Don't. Jump. But she's numb from the cold, growing apathetic, ashamed of herself, too, I should hope. See, nothing really makes a difference in my mother's case. Streetcars firecracker, skies burn, doors melt in the mind, but everything always returns to this: her, Nick, and tedium on the rebound. Quite right too — at least you know where you are, on the rebound.

Beaten, my mother returns to her bench, her penalty bench here in penalty park. She waits Nick out — Nick's dangerous fun stops being fun when my mother's head droops, drops, her gaze fixed on the tips of her boots and nowhere near Nick's glorious but unwatched jumps. He retires, unhurt, from the field, and begins to kick at a patch of dirty, old snow. The bench under my mother's bum has refrozen in her absence. Now, the bench thaws again. The seat of her pants soaks up the cold moisture. Another reason never to move again.

Nick sidles over to the swing set, and pushes idly at a swing. — Mommy, help. Mommy? The swing moves, comes close to hitting Nick in the head. Now she must move, tear herself (literally) from the bench.

— Careful, Nick. Wait. Hang on.

She lifts Nick into the too-small infant seat — stuffs him in. Never made for snowsuits, these bucket seats with their tongue-threatening iron bars. Maeve lifts the bar over Nick, pushes him down so she can clear his head, lowers the bar with a clang. A second later my brother finds himself airborne, fighting the wicked wind. He laughs and tries to look over his shoulder at his mother. Nick grins, shows his small white teeth. — More? says my mother. Shivers.

Slowly, down the sidewalk toward the park, someone comes, a tall figure, striding easily. A smaller shape moves smoothly beside the larger; they seem connected. Interest flutters deep in the centre of us. What do we have here? A hand-holding polar parent and child? Another twosome as desperate as Maeve and Nick? The pair comes closer, gains definition, coalesces into something recognizable. My mother's bleary lenses focus, tell the story. A fur hat for the tall shape. Four legs for the smaller. A coat for the human and four Velcro booties for his best friend. A man out walking his dog — a big, blond animal with a sharp nose and a curling tail. An exotic breed. A breed too new to name. A breed from distant climes. But still, a lot better adapted than my mother.

— Doggie, notes Nick, as the pair approaches.

They draw up alongside us, appear just over the fence that separates the park from the sidewalk. The man looks over at my mother, at my brother swinging in his swing. — Cold today, he says, steam issuing from his mouth. Then he smiles though the vapour. My mother smiles too, nods. Pushes Nick with an easy motion.

The man speaks confidently, says, — But the weather should be changing.

A minute later, when the jingle-jangle of the dog's collar and the sound of his master's steps fade away, my mother lifts Nick from the swing. — That's enough, she tells him. She's done. She's completely warm again: a few kind words, a bit of exercise pushing Nick, all she needed to relight the pilot light of her heart, to start the warm gusts of air through the pipes and vents, heating the spare parts of her, the empty rooms. She warms up places I never use, rooms empty save for a suitcase under a bed. A waste of space really. A waste of heat. A window left dangerously open, and who knows what could blow in? A cold wind down her neck could come in through my French doors, blow across my terrace, snatch at my big, floppy hat. Two entities, my mother and my house, but still, contiguities exist, and I've warned her about the drafts. All things considered, tedium is safer: this is Gerbil's point of view. Keep insides inside. Leave windows unopened. Doors closed.

Ø

My mother tries Darcy's door again after dinner. Again she knocks and again she holds the comics carefully in her free hand. Nick approves of the visiting, the knocking, but I don't. And I can't do anything to stop her. I'm a Gerbil under glass, floating in my displeasure dome. I'm peeking out from under her shirt. That's me there, the sulky one, the furry one with the shiny eyes. In my mother-bubble there's another bubble, one that hangs above my head — a thought-bubble with a single word. The word is, Don't.

She does. She knocks. And she knocks again. And just as she's turning back to our own apartment — just as I can begin to relax — the door opens with a burst of strangely familiar sound. Darcy stands there, wearing a shirt full of holes and an enormous pair of overalls. She eyes my mother, seems, well, disturbed.

Well, I'm not glad to see her. I've said it before, I'll say it again: Darcy's not sweet. I want my opinion on record. Knock-knocking's a bad idea. We don't see eye to eye on the subject of Darcy, me and Maeve. You know the song: I say pyjamas, tomato. My mother says Darcy.

— Hi.

— Hello.

When I see her — when I see Darcy — my displeasure, my discomfort, stings like a cold wind, like air from outside. Let me make it loud and clear. I don't sanction my mother's mouth grinning. I can't approve the wiggling of her toes. Her legs displease me, her back makes me deeply uneasy. So do her butt, her breasts. Her arms right down to her fingers are unsatisfactory. Her face has always been her own and she can have what's on the other side of the brain barrier — god knows, I've never wanted *that*. But I want what's mine. She and I have a prenatal agreement: from fundus to pubis. A Gerbil's home is my castle. In the case of a separation, the house is mine.

Separation? I didn't say that. Who said that?

— What's up?

— Your drawings, your books. I wanted to ... I read them.

Darcy's face changes, smiles from the dimples in her chin to the barrettes on her head. Bi-i-i-g smile — god, how I hate her.

— You read them?

— I *love* them.

Darcy invites her in. Of course she does. Who wouldn't.

Ø

Darcy holds the door open for my mother. My mother steps forward then pauses. She stands on the threshold, shuffles her feet. Decides. — Um ... I wanted to show you something first, my mother tells Darcy. — Sort of a trade for what you showed me. It's nothing like that, but, well, given the ... um, subject matter (she giggles — god, she giggles), I thought — I hoped — you might be interested.

Here's me, Mom. Pulling my own short hair. Chewing on my lip. Stamping my own little feet with agony. Here's my plea: oh god, spare me my mother's drawing. Pencilled incoherence. Skimpy sketches. Graphite violence.

— What? says Darcy. My mother hands her a sheet of paper.

— Me see, says Nick.

Nick grabs Darcy's wrist and pulls down her hand far enough to allow him a peek at the image she holds. Darcy lets him because she's looking at my mother with an expression I just can't make out. For all my mother squints and stares, we can't make out what she's thinking.

— What is it?

— Look.

Darcy gently frees her wrist from Nick and looks again. — I don't know what this is, she says. She holds out the paper square and it's not what I thought. It's a photocopied image — a black and white square.

— It's of the ultrasound, says my mother.

— You mean, this is your baby?

My mother nods.

Darcy looks up. Tries to hand back the picture, but my mother links her fingers over her belly. Darcy shrugs, looks down at the picture again. — I don't even see a baby, says Darcy. — Are you sure there's one there?

— Da'cy, says Nick and tries to swing on her legs.

— Cut it out, says my mother distractedly as she bends her head to look at the picture Darcy holds out. She points with her finger. — Head there. Spine. Bum. Darcy squints. — Eye socket, says my mother.

— Oh, says Darcy suddenly. — Oh! A knee. An elbow.

— Arm there. Other arm down near the legs.

— Oh my God, says Darcy, a baby.

— Bum, says Nick.

They bend down together until their heads are almost touching. I don't sanction this bending, this almost touching. I don't sanction this sharing of me with virtual strangers, not even this paparazzi snapshot. I don't remember having this likeness taken. Taken — the word says everything necessary. Is my fur combed? My face washed? This picture was taken. And unsanctioned.

— Look at the hand ... all clenched up.

— A fist. Sure. I see the — what's this?

— What's what?

— Oh my god, says Darcy again.

— What?

— Hard to say. 's like looking at a broken television.

— Tee-vee? says Nick hopefully.

My mother looks at Darcy. Frowning.

— Oh my, says Darcy, beginning to laugh.

— What?!

My mother tries to take the paper from Darcy but Darcy seems interested for real now, hangs on tight.

— Look again, Maeve. The bumps. Knuckles. Count them from here. One ... two ...

— Hang on. I can't see that well. I see one ... two ...

— See ...

— Looks like a ...

— Like a *middle* finger.

Ø

Oh ho. I *hate* Darcy. I like to think I'm an eloquent Gerbil, but there are no words for how I hate her stupid hair, her crop tops, her piercings, her 'tats.' I hope her labia ring pustulates (she's sure to have one). I hope her cell phone leaks battery acid in her pocket. Her iPod volume spirals out of control. I hope ... I hope ...

No, no ... I *know*. I hope she grows up and has *babies*.

Ø

Darcy shepherds us through her door, closes it behind us. I feel a little giddy, looking at hallways, doors, rooms curving in the wrong direction. I know where we are: Wonderland. Nothing's going to go right from here on in. I could kick my mother. I could warn her. But I won't. I can't. My mother's on her own.

There's a boy in Darcy's hallway. He's come out of the kitchen to check out the disruption. Light from Darcy's widdershins window filters though the hall, blue and smoky. In the dimness I take a moment to understand what the boy is doing with the box he holds in his big hands. He's scooping cereal into his mouth, crunching, chewing. He smiles at Darcy. Darcy smiles back.

—Where's Nick, says my mother. Nick has escaped from her grasp, disappeared into the apartment as surely as if he knew where he was going—which he does, in a way.

—Who's this, asks the boy in Darcy's hallway. He takes a long look at my mother. My mother looks at the floor, but I say, Look, Maeve. Won't kill you to take a good long look. Go on. Meet his eyes. Stare him down. He's laughing at you, with your bulbous belly, your pendulous paps. Don't put up with that shit. Look back. Stare. Check out the spotty chin, the singleton eyebrow. Let your eyes bounce off that Adidas T-shirt, tight and flat. Jesus. Cereal-boy's flexing his muscles just for you, Mom, tossing back handfuls of Cheerios. Bet he can't catch one between his teeth. Stare at him. Let him know that he doesn't worry you. C'mon, Mom, don't be a doormat.

But, of course, she's the world's fattest doormat, unable to lie flat. A flabby foot-wiper. She gives me canted, nervous Nellie views of hallway, floor, ceiling. The arch of the living room slips into view, freezes full frame. A blink. A cut. A neat reverse of Darcy's face, still smiling.

— Where's Nick, says my mother, and her voice sounds flat, deadened by the proximity of her walls to my nose. I could lick her insides like a Popsicle. I'm thinking I'm *much* bigger than I was.

— In there, says Darcy, pointing. My mother follows her finger under the arch and into the living room where Nick crouches, very small in front of a giant television. He's a pixel-edged shadow between my mother and the glowing screen. My mother follows Nick's gaze to where St. Bugs capers and wisecracks. St. Bugs is tremendous, loud, unmistakable.

— Gerb'l, says Nick.

Nick, I've got to tell you I'm flattered, my brother, but fear you're mistaken. That rodent on screen is a hero of mine. A relation even. But, no, my ears are shorter and closer to the skull. My nose more roman in profile. My tail is long and slender. Like a finger. No powder-puff on the butt for me.

— Hey Nick, calls Darcy. — You like cartoons, huh.

Nick fails to answer. Squats, excessively rapt.

— Yes, he does, says my mother, and they both look at the television. There's a bull on screen now, Bugs in a toreador's three-cornered hat. The bull makes a run at Bugs; there's an anvil behind Bug's cape. — What a Maroon, says the tricky rabbit. — What a Gulli-bull.

Nick laughs, rolling on the floor. Laughs and laughs. Darcy laughs at Nick. — Hey, she says. — He might wet his pants, but, anyway, they're diapers.

— Gul'bull, says Nick, eyes never leaving the screen.

— Sit down, says Darcy, and immediately throws herself onto a soft, clean sofa. The boy joins her, wraps himself behind, arms up her shirt as if his hands are cold. I feel sick. Is it just me?

My mother says something from the doorway to the room. —The volume's a little loud, she says, but nobody hears her. The bull has swallowed a rifle, is shooting out his horns. BANG. BANG. Everyone else is laughing. —The volume, repeats my mother. This time the boy hears her. He looks at her blankly, takes off his baseball cap, rolls the brim between his hands. He smiles at her.

—What's your name, asks the boy. My mother tells him.—Well, y'know, Maeve, he says digging deep in a thigh pocket. —Now that you're here ... (dig, dig) you might as well sit down ... (dig) and ... (dig, dig) get out of the doorway.

My mother watches what he's pulling out of his pocket, what he's lining up on the wooden table in front of him. —That's okay, she says, sighing. —We have to go now. Nick.

The boy sets out his lighter, his papers, his bag of hydroponic dope. How do I know it's hydroponic? He tells us; he says so, grinning at my mother as he drops the baggie with a plop on Darcy's little table. God, he's so young —practically Nick-like. He doesn't know what he's doing —messes with the rolling paper, can't get the line to run straight and even. Fumbles, spills all over Darcy's table. I'm as surprised as the next Gerbil when my mother's hands shoot into the picture. Get the feeling she's kind of surprised as well. Certainly the boy looks at her with his mouth open.

—I can't stand it, she says to him. Dumping the dope back into his baggie, she smoothes out the crumpled paper and begins again, rolling him a lovely little blunt the size of Nick's pinky.

—Christ, says the boy. Darcy laughs.

—Now we *really* have to go, says Maeve.

Ø

My mother has hurried Nick into the hall, a bum's rush for the door. Halfway there, neurons fire, synapses light up, Nick figures out he's going home — away from the 'tee-vee'. He opens his mouth, turns red. A howl splits the air, knees loosen. Nick goes limp — save a pillar of angry, vibrating sound that animates his core. Maeve finds herself dragging her stiff son and stops. She doesn't know that Darcy is right behind her. Darcy bumps into my mother, my mother staggers, almost falls over Nick. More slapstick, this. I like it fine.

— Don't go, yet, says Darcy, when she's untangled herself from Nick and my mother. — I want to show you something.

My mother hesitates, then picks up Nick. My brother, the genius, still incandesces with rage, but now he's mad because everyone fell on him. — Ged off, shouts Nick. Ged aaawff!

— I am off, Nick. Shhh. You're okay.

Darcy helps. — Show me your leg, Nick, she shouts. Surprised, my brother stares at her. She looks stern. — Leg. Nick sticks out one stubby limb. Darcy takes his shoe and gives the leg a jiggly shake. — Hmmm, she says, giving it another shake. — Looks all right. Next. Nick holds out his other leg, half strangling my mother in the process. Darcy shakes this leg. — Hmmm, she says. — No good at all. Nick's lower lip begins to tremble. — Stop that, says Darcy, quite gently, really. — I can fix it. Come with me, Nick.

We all follow Darcy, away from the entrance and down the hall. Three of us on one pair of feet, sinking deep into the rug.

Darcy stops in front of the door that corresponds to Nick's room in my mother's apartment. She half turns and gives us a conspiratorial wink before pushing open the door. Aimed at?... Nick? My mother? Me? And I remember to hate Darcy again. Not to be charmed like my snot-nosed brother, my lonely mother.

Darcy's studio, of course. Much better light than on our side of the building. Even. Clear. The room has few furnishings: an old chair, a bookcase, an Anglepoise lamp, a drawing table positioned at the spot where all our eyes collect.

— Oh, says my mother, in a pleased voice. Oh.

— I'm working on the next bit now, says Darcy. Smug. Smiling Darcy. Snot-nosed too, in her own way.

— Oh, says my mother. She's afraid to step even further into the room. Nick begins to wriggle in her arms, working himself free of her grasp. His feet catch me a blow on my west wall, knock plaster loose, bounce a few healthy blood cells off my mantelpiece where I'd set them for safekeeping. — No, Nick.

Darcy remembers her promise to Nick. Looks at him gravely, says, — I'm going to fix you, Nick.

If only she would. If only she could. Would I forgive her then? Not in a million years. I hate this Darcy, standing at her drawing table selecting a thin-tipped felt pen from a plastic ice cream carton filled with pens, pencils, paintbrushes. I can feel Maeve salivating. Drool puddles in my hallways, fills my play pool. Stop. Enough. I have a bad feeling about all this. My anxiety grows as Darcy digs for a scrap of paper and begins to draw, screening what she's doing with her hand. As she works, she talks to Nick, says, — Nick. This will fix you, Nick. Wait 'til you see what I can do.

— Me see, says Nick, relaxing in my mother's arms.

— Wait, greedy, says Darcy.

My mother edges closer, as if to give Nick a better look at the busy, drawing Darcy. In fact, Maeve's got eyes for the surface of the drawing table. She's hungry for scraps. Not much to feast on — a single sheet of drawing paper lies on the table, covered neatly with another. But Darcy, in finding the paper scrap for Nick, has knocked the covering page askew; the corner of the page below shows. My mother sees the hand drawn edge of one frame and its contents: a jawline (I know it immediately), half a pair of lips (the curve unmistakable), part of a nose (can she miss it, again?). Darcy's pen scritches, scratches. My mother shifts closer to the table, frowns in concentration. She shifts Nick to her other arm and reaches out toward the hidden page.

— There, says Darcy, finishing her drawing for Nick, holding it up for us to see.

My mother starts, stops dead, her free hand still outstretched. Darcy sees her and gives her a look I can't read. Why can't I read this Darcy? She's no literary classic. Pulp. Beach fare. She's a *comic book* for god's sake. Coolly, Darcy stares Maeve down and holds out her drawing for Nick to see. On cue, Nick gurgles, bugles, trumpets his pleasure. We all turn to look at Darcy's drawing. Maeve hardly sees the slickness of the lines, the certainty of the shapes. She swallows hard. Darcy doesn't seem to notice, caught up in Nick's pleasure. Darcy gives Nick her skilful little sketch of Bugs Bunny.

—Gerb'l, says Nick.

No. No. No, I say. Why won't anyone listen?

Ø

Bedtime comes, goes. Night sags, falls, as usual. Always does —a blessing of sorts. The apartment suffers under the weight of my mother's sad domesticity. Frown lines run the length of the narrow kitchen, burdened by half-washed laundry. Nick's sodden pants. Tiny socks. Shirts with arms outstretched. Stop. But the water torture proceeds: drips up and down the lino with no rhythm, no regularity. No order. The sink sinks under dirty dishes. A jar of pasta sauce sits in a puddle of former contents —a scene from a horror film. A crusty spoon lies nearby. The murder weapon.

My mother stands, squeezed between the washer and the sink. Nick calls from his bedroom but she's pretending not to hear. Gingerly, she reaches out, tries the handle of the spoon. Disobedient. Refuses to come to her hand.

—Mommy?

Nick stands on the threshold with his covers draped around his head. Another ghost. He says —Want Daddy. Oh Daddy. His eyes are blue, black-lashed. My father, an everlasting bruise, rising though the skin. My mother sighs.

—Mommy? says Nick. —Bed? P'ease.

Five minutes later, Nick squirms, wriggles in my mother's bed, twitches while he waits for sleep. Kicks her. Kicks me. A dispassionate boot between ribs — who knows whose. My mother rolls over, presents her back to the soles of Nick's feet. Still he wiggles, twitches, covers my mother with accidental thumps to shoulders, to buttocks from heel and toe. A reflex. Nick kicks her — not black, not blue, not even close. She falls asleep waiting for Mahon to call.

But just before my mother's lights go out, she shifts in bed, brushes accidental lips against her own forearm. Instinctively, she kisses the soft skin she finds there. Baby limbs, backs of heads, grubby fingers suffering booboos have conditioned her day after day to purse lips on contact, to kiss all and everything in her path. I am obliged to notice that her love has learned to lack discernment, has come to include, just for a moment, herself.

ALARM BELLS. FIRE. FLOOD. MURDER.

The telephone wakes us up, Maeve and I. Blank eyeballs roll and flutter. Maeve in bed, an empty snake's skin, a vacant caddis fly husk. A twitch. A shudder. The corpse comes back to life. And we're home.

— Whos'zat?

— Maeve, it's me.

It's him.

— Whazza time?

— Late.

— 's too late.

One of us — both of us? our body on its own? — wants to go back to sleep.

— Maeve.

She's a bit more awake now. Understands what's going on. — Fell asleep, she says, slightly apologetically, as if she shouldn't do this at night. She pulls this lump of a body upright, props us against a pillow. Finds Nick wedged beside her, mercifully still asleep. — You okay?

— Maeve, says my father. You don't know what it's like up here.

— I know.

— No, you don't.

— Yes, I do, she says. Inhibition sleeps on, allows her mouth to go solo. — You get to stay up late. You get to sleep in. You get to eat out. You go out for drinks.

— 's not like that.

— Yes, it is.

— Then why do I want to come home so bad?

— God, I don't know. Why ask me?

My father sighs. Looking for sympathy. For a good cry, call M-a-e-v-e. — Take tonight, he says. — Tonight, all I could think of was you guys ...

chapter eight

— What? You're mumbling.

— Did Nick ask for me at bedtime?

— Not a word.

— Not even ...

— He's little. He forgets pretty quick.

Mahon makes a low, keening sound. My mother cuts him off. She's waking up fast. Brighter all the time. — Well, maybe he asked a little, I don't know. It was hours ago — what time is it anyway? Is it night or morning? My mother cranes her head to see the glowing red numbers of the desk clock. — Oh god, it's 5:14 in the morning.

— There's no damn clock in here.

My mother snorts, rolls her eyes. — Where are you?

— Lakeshore Inn.

— I mean, where?

— It's a motel....

— Never mind. What's that noise? Dave's there, isn't he.

— We've been talking.

— Oh god.

— Yeah well.

— Yeah nothing.

— Dave's got some new ideas. That's what I wanted to tell you, Maeve. Dave says if I stick out the band he's going to call in some favours, friends and friends of friends ... and stuff.

— You're his only friend, Mahon. No one else can stand him.

— People he knows in the industry.

— Oh ... The Industry.

— He says he's got an A&R guy who wants to hear us live. They heard a tape... they're interested, Maeve.

My mother says nothing.

— They're *interested.*

— You're a bar band, Mahon. Nobody's interested.

— 's not true. We've got our own stuff. Dave's remixed the songs.

— Uh-huh.

—They liked what they heard.

—Mahon, you guys have done all this already.

—Yeah, but that was before.

—Before what?

—Our sound, Maeve. It's going to be huge.

—Mahon, can we afford this call?

—A monster sound.

—Go to bed.

—Is Nick there? Let me talk to Nick.

—He's asleep, Mahon. Remember? It's the middle of the night.

—Just tell Nick, a monster sound. He'll like that.

—Whatever.

—Tell him tomorrow.

—I have to go.

—Maeve ...

—Okay, I'll tell him.

—Maeve ...

—No. Enough.

My father's breathing takes on a husky, furry intonation in my mother's echo chambers. She weakens his signal. He weakens hers.

—Go to sleep, she tells him at last.

—I'm really fucking tired.

—So go to sleep.

—Is it light there?

—I don't want to know.

—Where are you? On the hall phone?

—No.

—On the bedroom phone?

—Well, it's next to the bed, Mahon. Where I sleep.

—Why are you hissing?

—I'm not hissing. I'm whispering. Nick's asleep beside me.

—Yeah? Well, I got *Dave* here next to me.

—Congratulations. May you have many happy years of wedded bliss.

— He snores.

— But good in bed I bet.

— I've had better.

— You rock gods are such sluts.

— Is it light there?

— Maybe a little pink in the sky. Just, like, one cloud.

— One cloud, huh.

— Well, it's just kind of streaky. Everywhere else is pitch black.

— Is it raining?

— No. It's been nice.

— Stores opening yet? The signs on?

— I'd have to get up to see. Too early, I think.

— The traffic ... is the traffic?... Mahon yawns in my mother's ear.

— You're falling asleep.

— I can't sleep without you.

— Yes, you can.

Mahon yawns again.

— See.

— Maeve.

— What?

— I love you.

— Yeah yeah.

— I do.

— Yeah.

— I'd come home anytime, you know I would.

— You're scaring me, Mahon.

— I'm not saying I will. Just that I would.

— Get paid first.

— I love you.

— Hmmm.

— Aw, just say it, Maeve. Then I'll go. I'll get off the phone. I promise.

— ...

— Please.

— ...

— I love you, Maeve. Please say it. ...No, no, don't cry.

But my mother can't help herself. She blubbers helplessly into the phone. She stutters over 'I.' She snivels out 'love.' Her mouth collapses around 'you' and she howls like a dog. She waters; she weeps. And at the height of the fuss she puts out a finger from the burrow of blankets she's made for herself, and presses down on the disconnect. She holds until there's a mark on the tip of her finger, a little red ring. Then she releases. Listens. The line's dead. My father's gone.

The window's dark grey. No pinky streak. There isn't a shred of pink in the sky. My mother cries light into the sky. She cries up the sound of morning traffic in the slush. She cries the shop signs switched on, their doors open.

Should I cry too? Well I won't. Tired of taking her part — don't say I haven't. I've been sympathetic. She's the one who doesn't get it.

Going back to bed.

∅

Wake up with sick on my rug — a beautiful rug with its blood-red figured knots that cord like muscle across the room. Now there's a stain near the middle — beige, lumpy, concealing and congealing. Don't need a doctor to diagnose this mess. This mess is puke. Spew. Upchuck. I want to do something — throw open windows, let light flood in, let smell slink out, but there are no windows which open in my red room, no windows at all. Only shutters. Only long-lashed blinds.

An eye-shade. A window-lid. A tattered screen between here and there. Pixel memories. My mother and Nick lift like ghosts into blue sky. The sun explodes, burns. Grass grows greener beneath hothouse heat. Greener and greener and greener. I shut my eyes — a reasonable response to the things I see. Inky jawline. Curve of lips. I won't open my eyes. I won't.

I don't. But with eyes shut, orientation takes time, takes cunning. I'm sick of Maeve's bifurcated vision. Return me, please, to subsonic rumblings. To undersea songs. Away from the twined, twinned, looped aural channels. Let me sink back fathoms, down where treasures lie: wordless voices. Other sounds too. Clumps. Bangs. A fibrillating whoosh. My brother Nick, reduced to footfalls. The sound of distressed metal. Sighs, only so much wind whistling through this domed chamber.

Working blind takes cunning. And cunning orientation works like this: I set my brother-sounds at polar north. East and west sit soft chairs, randomly squeaking. South is the slapping of files, sharp-sided on a desk. My mother swings like a needle, points in turn to all directions, points at last to the answer, the sum of coordinates: the doctor's office. And at the centre of every compass lies the best direction of all, the hub and the heart. Inside is a point, too, where sits Gerbil waiting with ears pricked, waiting for the doctor, waiting for a clean bill of health.

Not bad with eyes shut, huh?

Now my mother rises from those squeaking chairs, removes me from the waiting room — carefully carries her Gerbil as if I were blind. As if. I'm not blind, not even with my eyes closed. This room, as we enter, is waiting for me. Space unfilled presses lightly in on the fluid filled chamber of my head. My pricked ears return sounds and soundings alike, echoes that bounce though thick air. With eyes closed, I see four tight corners, four more tucked under the ceiling. Hmmm, an outside kind of room with echoes both hard and sharp. The colour scheme — I don't need to open eyes — is beige. A weigh scale. Growth charts on the wall. A room for asking monosyllabic questions, recording monosyllabic answers. A nurse enters behind us (click-clack), sits at my mother's side, digging. Writes with a pencil (scritch-scratch). The pink nipple of the eraser waves, stirs the air like soup. The nurse punctuates her song-like sentences with pauses. My mother grunts, moans, whines in response. I open my ears just a tiny bit more, hear the whole thing. A sample question: When did you last feel the baby moving?

— Oh ... this morning. I had some juice.

Did it move vigorously?

— Yes.

How many times?

— Um, lots?

My mother thinks she has all the answers — answers pour out of her. Sometimes her voice rises, eager, hopeful, wanting to please. Longer answers stutter forward, finish in a rush. Listen for the nodding of the nurse's head in the thick air. Listen for the tilt of her head. Listen for the rhythm of that rubber nipple.

The nurse finishes her questions, settles pencil on desk. Thunk.

— So ... is everything okay? asks my mother.

Everything? Anything? Okay with the mother of discontent, brooding over a big belly? Okay when the skies are always sour overhead, weeping vinegar milk? Let hope pluck at your vocal cords, lift the untied ends of your sentences. Let your voice trail.... Let it full stop. Breathe. Sigh. Tremble even. But don't ask if everything's okay.

I whack my mother with my fist, fully fingerprinted. Sometimes, after french fries and ketchup, spicy chicken wings, pizza, I find whorls of grease on windows and walls. Now when I press hard into her guts, I leave fingerprints as clues — visible evidence of a Gerbil's frustration, the pokes and jabs of irritation, the full body gouges of utter exasperation. I reach up (no need to stretch), leave a fist-sized impression in the ceiling just above my head. A permanent dent to add to my collection. Souvenirs of tantrums, of hissy fits. But if my mother feels me now she stays dumb; my mother *is* dumb. A maroon. So gullible. No matter, the bigger I get the harder I hit. And I'm big now. Heavy dents in the plaster. Deep dints in the wallboard. Notches in the moulding. Nicks in the floorboards.

Nicks? Where's Nick?

Ø

This bit doesn't help. Doesn't seem to — doesn't quite fit.

— Everything all right?

— What?

— Did the nurse say anything?

— No.

— Is that pee in that cup?

— Yes.

— Oh.

Ø

The nurse comes back again. — Mrs. Mahon. The doctor will see you. Maeve gets heavily to her feet.

— Nick?

Nick explodes from his chair. Dancing thuds, snorts of baby breath. No one even tries to catch him. — Come on, says Nick's mother.

The nurse puts out a hand, stops my mother. — Mrs. Mahon. Mrs. Mahon, leave your sample with me please. Thank you, Mrs. Mahon. To the left please. No, your other left.

My mother treads heavily. She over-pronates. Not good in a runner. Worse in a mother. In an undertone, she complains about her back, her pelvis. She rubs her tailbone, tries to stretch out her over-taut muscles.

The examination room has softer chairs than the place we saw the nurse. Maeve sinks into one. My room flattens out — pressure again. Nick climbs into her lap, leaning against her belly. My brother's a big boy. He makes waves in my sea, induces rocking. At least the sensation of moving water soothes. Eyes still shut, my room has faded to the non-colour of liquid darkness. Maeve sways. Nick provides counterweight, loosely follows her lead, always a moment behind. They rock. A lot of time flows past. Hard for a Gerbil to keep track. Look for my watch but find it hard to move my hand, caught in some soft fold, some invisible biomass. I struggle. Get my wrist free. No watch. Left at home. How long will all this take?

Ø

A squeak. No, not me squeaking, not Gerbil. A door. A door and a voice. The doctor, in heels, taps her way across the room, makes a chair creak, sits. She greets my mother. A short silence comes next, and then my mother startles all by sniffing. Once. Then, she just shuffles into tears. A slow tap dance (a plunk and a plonk). Speeding up. Syncopating now (pitter-patter). Finally, rapid-fire raindrops.

— Kleenex? says the doctor.

— Thank you.

A tissue rips from the dry cardboard box. A shy nose blow. Wipe, wipe.

— Do you have a garbage?

Ø

What comes next? This bit.

— Did you get weighed? Where's your blood pressure?

Nick yawns. His mother leans forward. — On the other page. The sound of paper turning.

— Oh, there it is.

Ø

Then this bit. How does it go? Same voice as the last bit — that doctor.

— No, you've a right to feel this way.

...

— No, that's not unreasonable.

...

— You need to talk with him.

...

— Kleenex?

Pay attention, Gerbil. Wake up. Open your eyes. Look. This is me, slapping my cheeks. Trying to wake myself up. Waking myself up. Things are happening.

Convexities form overhead, my ceiling droops doubly. The doctor shifts her hands, palpitating inches from my head. She presses and probes, hunts me down. — Here, she says, pausing. — Here ... here ... and here. The doctor cups her hands, uses her forearms to confirm, describe, limit. Straightening, she gently touches her index finger to my vault — a more modest version of the Sistine Chapel. A bump forms where she presses. She lifts her hand, hovers, lowers her finger again to sketch a skinny, waggling line that threatens to tickle. Such a little line. Such a perfect shape. The doctor crooks her finger. There's an itch in that finger. She sketches again the baby whose outline cools on a bare acre of skin — an invisible infant, curved like an ear that listens intently between fundus and pubis.

— Oh, that's fine, says the doctor. — Nick? Should we listen to the baby today? Nick agrees. The doctor's heels tap-tap on the floor. Something metal moves. I hear the sweet hum of electricity.

— The gel will be a little cold, says the doctor.

Brace myself. For a moment or two there's only silence. Then a whooshing sound, a swishing sound.

— Ooooh.

— Hmmm, says the doctor.

Electricity hums louder. Now there's a sucking noise as well as the whooshing — an aortic slurping, in and out. A flurry of heartbeats.

— There, Nick. Hear it?

— Hear it? Hear the baby?

Go on, Nick. Your party piece. 'Erbil. Say it, Nick. Say Gerbil.

— Baby.

Ø

My brother. Ain't he cute. What a sweet little man.

You think? You don't know the half of it. After the doctor's office, my mother takes Nick shopping. Across town to the big stores. Eyes wide open this time.

Nick's stroller rolls easily off the streetcar into the underground station. From there a row of glass doors leads into the basement of the big store. Earlier, a few anxious moments about the stroller and streetcar almost scuppered the trip. But now we've arrived safely, passed through the doors. Wide aisles. Solid footing. Bright lights. We whiz through the hall, my mother stretching her legs as far as they can go, Nick bouncing in the stroller.

The escalator wears a warning sign: a silhouette child (blocky and obedient) stands independently, holds his mother's silhouette hand. My mother knows better — knows Nick. No silhouette he. Full colour. Better off staying in his stroller, safely under lock and key. Maeve times her forward surge, sets the stroller's front wheels squarely on a step, allows the rising stair to lift the front wheels until she can safely set the back wheel down on a lower stair. Nick gazes straight up into her face. — Wheee, Nick, says Maeve. — Up we go. Nick says nothing.

Up, up we go. All the way to the lingerie department. A sinuous woman greets us at the top of the stairs. Tall and bald, Amazonian, she twists, drops one shoulder, carries one hand on her hip. Her black teddy slips off her shoulder, while a garter belt and net stockings cover her firm flesh. A feather boa encircles her plastic neck. My mother shakes her head. As if. And pushes us past the pole dancing panties, toward the back of the department where the housecoats hang in hairy, unsexy formation.

Housecoats — why we're here. Well, Maeve anyway. I don't need a housecoat, have a fine furry coat already. Nick (who has the purple snowsuit) and I just came along for the ride. Maeve stops, fingers terry towel, velour, cotton, before debating the merits, demerits, of each. Then she fingers them each again. To her bulging bod, she holds them: floor-length, calf-long, thigh-high. Shakes her head again, especially at this last one, and puts them all back on the rack. Begins her fingering again, this time price tags, washing instructions, country of manufacture.

Nick gets bored of this pretty quickly, doesn't think much of her efforts to be thrifty, careful, or responsible — to hell with shopping, my brother. Nick begins to rock in his stroller, thrusts out his tum with increasing violence until the wheels threaten to lift off the floor. Maeve takes the stroller handles, pushes Nick back and forth, shushes him. Oh, long time since that worked, Nick's mother. Long time. Nick throws himself from side to side, uttering a shriek to the left, shriek to the right. — Out (right side). — Out (left side). — Outoutout.

Maeve succumbs to my brother's particular logic. Nick is freed. Maeve lifts the sleeve of a bathrobe, feels terry towel between her fingers.

Nick is lost.

Maeve sighs, drapes three of her first choice bathrobes over the empty stroller and goes in search of Nick. She rolls up and down the aisle, calm at first, then increasingly frantic. — Nicky, she calls, trying in vain to control her voice.

Soon, an older woman with her hands full of pyjamas joins in the search. Comes back immediately with a little girl. Tear-shaped pigtails. Brown eyes that look up at Maeve wonderingly. Maeve only hesitates a second before shaking her head. On cue, the child's real mother parts a rack of pyjamas, steps through and claims her child. Like in a comedy routine. Ha ha. This mother only laughs at the flustered apologies, tells them she knows they didn't mean to steal her child. — Oh, I had my eye out, she tells them, magisterially unconcerned with possible kidnapping. Sweeping her little daughter along with her, she sails away, one eye (or both), presumably, still out. My mother, most manifestly, should keep her eye out too, worn like snail's eyes on two little stalks. Or sewn on her shoulders like epaulettes.

—Here's Nick, Mommy, cries Nick, popping out from the middle of a rack of sale items. He's pulled down a couple of giant nude-coloured garments and hidden himself under them. A great game.

My mother, I'm afraid, doesn't agree. Shouts. Oh yes, she shouts. She shouts until the woman who tried to help disappears, unthanked, unnoticed, uncomfortable, as my mother keeps on shouting.

ø

My mother takes her housecoats to the changing rooms. She pulls Nick by one hand, steers the stroller with the other. The stroller yaws wildly, fetches up on both sides of the corridor leading to her cubicle, while my mother pushes, stalls, reverses, pushes again. At last she gets everything inside: housecoats, stroller, Nick, herself, Gerbil. Crammed in. Sardines staring at ourselves in the shiny lid of our can. Housecoats. Stroller. Nick. Herself. Gerbil. Face to flipper and packed in oil. Still, my mother begins to try on her housecoats, as jammed into her room as I am in mine. We stretch out an arm and rap our knuckles. Step sideways and bang our hip. And she's prone to sudden movements, my mother. Knee-jerk reactions to the sight of herself in the mirror. Starts of horror. Dismay. None of the housecoats looks good. All cost more than she wants to pay. Draped in the last, she turns this way and that, checking out her enormous bum. Her profile looks almost indistinguishable from her front view.

Depressed, Maeve takes off the garment and looks one more time at us all in the mirror: housecoats, stroller, herself, and Gerbil. Sits down on the newly vacated bench behind her and puts her head in her hands.

What's in that head of hers that she should take hold of it so carefully? Why, there's an answer nestled in her head. And what's the question to that answer? The question is what's gone missing from the mirror? Let's take a look: housecoat, stroller, mother, Gerbil ...

Nick. Again. Nick's gone missing.

This time, though, he reappears almost instantly, climbing back under the low partition to the cubicle with practiced ease. He holds something in his hands, something huge and floppy, lacy, nude in colour. Maeve takes whatever it is from Nick and unfolds his find. A pair of underpants. Held against her waist, they're even too big for my mother. She begins to laugh. Sinks back to the bench.

— Are these for Mommy, Nick? she asks as soon as she can speak again.

Nick shakes his head. No.

— Not for Mommy?

(No.)

— For Nicky?

(Big shake of his head — negative.)

— Are you sure? says my mother. — I think you might look nice in these ugly undies. She tries to hold the pants up against Nick but he pushes her hands away. She could cover three Nicks with this expanse of fabric. She flaps the underpants like a matador. — Better than Batman underpants, Nick, she says. — Better than Spider-man. She begins to chant Ugly Undies. Ugly Undies.

Laughing, made good-humoured by her own juvenile jokes, my mother tosses away the ugly undies on her heap of discarded clothing. Her eye alights again on the bathrobes. Now that she thinks twice — now that she's had a vision of the ugly undies — the robes aren't really as bad as she'd thought. She drapes the best one over her arm. Leaves the rejected two behind on the bench. Shakes her head at them. — You've been a bad boy today, she says, dumping my brother, now curiously unresisting, into the stroller, strapping him in. — But *nothing's* as bad as the Ugly Undies.

With a final snort of childish laughter, my mother opens the door of her cubicle and comes face to face with a middle-aged woman who stands in the hallway holding her slacks bunched around her waist. Behind her, Maeve can see an open cubicle containing a neatly placed pair of boots. On the bench sits a pile of one-piece swimsuits. The woman looks uncomfortable, as if she weren't wearing any ...

Nick. What a little charmer. A real gentleman. And he's not done yet, my brother.

Ø

Maeve has one more stop to make before I can take my house and go home. She rolls Nick out into the steel and glass mall, steers him toward the drugstore — my mother finds the place vast and delightful. A real remedy for the embarrassments of the past hour. Drugstore goos, powders, jars, and bottles attract her eyes, her twitching nose. Maeve and Nick cruise the aisles filling her basket with things she needs. A new toothbrush. A new brush. A new comb. A small travel toothpaste. Nick follows behind her, also filling her basket. His small nose twitches too. When she comes to the gleaming cash desk, my mother obediently unloads everything onto the conveyor belt. With a grunt of satisfaction, she surveys her choices — her choices and so much more. A box of blond hair dye (where?). Three cakes of shaving soap (how?). An orange, twist-top container of hair pomade (d'oh). — Oh no, Nicky, no, no. Not this time you don't, she says.

Maeve deftly removes Nick's errant selections, smiling sweetly at the cashier as she does so. — We won't want these, she says. But Nick does. Nick wants them. Wants dem. Wants dem enough to make a fuss. No good. Nick's pots and jars must be abandoned. Nick's mother stands firm, even while bending over. Fussing. Patting. Soothing.

Later, on the streetcar home, my mother will smile to herself, remembering how Nick lost that round. Fifty-fifty. That's how she'll score the day. Nick scored a hit in round one, but round two is all hers. And everyone knows, winner takes all.

I say, It's okay, Nick. You and I know the truth. When she bent to fuss, pat, soothe, then — unbeknownst to her — she bought and paid for your final selection: a pair of cat's-eyed, rhinestone bedecked, purple sunglasses. She'll thank you for it too. Sure she will. Any minute now. She's on the streetcar now. She's got her hand in the bag. She's fingering her purchases.

Ø

Maeve stops at the mailbox on the way up to her apartment. Opens the little metal door with a key. Gets the same thrill every time. Inside is a phone bill, an offer for a credit card, and a postcard. Oxfordshire. She reads the message.

Stately homes! The bus drops us off at a new one every day. The gardens are fantastic. Roses like you wouldn't believe. And such a smell — so sweet. Twice the size of ours, even though ours give us some much needed colour in the front. Devonshire cream tea every afternoon. I swear, I can't eat another scone, no matter how tempting that naughty filling. Yum.

My mother can't read the signature, can't think who would be sending her such a message. She looks at the picture again. Rolling green hills. A church steeple off in the distance. The lettering a deep blue. Has some secret been hidden here? She reads over the message again. On a whim she takes the first letter of the first word of every sentence. STTRATDIY. Makes no sense. Finally, she thinks to check the address opposite the message. Three buildings down the block. The postcard isn't for her at all.

Her downstairs neighbour comes down the stairs to check her own box. Maeve shows her the card, telling the woman, — 's not for me at all.

— Well, set it on the radiator. Redirect it like.

— Will that work?

— Here. The lady from downstairs takes a red pen from somewhere behind her ear and circles the address once, very hard. She sets the postcard, address up, on the radiator. — There, she says. — Postie will see to that.

Maeve stands, strangely awed by the red pen, by the vigorous penmanship. She rests her hands on her protruding gut.

— Won't be long now, says the neighbour, replacing her pen and retrieving her own mail.

— No, says Maeve, still thinking of the postcard. — Tomorrow, I guess. He should be glad to get it. It's a nice message.

The neighbour gives Maeve a sharp look. Maeve can see the red tip of the pen just jutting out from behind a grey curl. Then the neighbour smiles. Only when she is upstairs and safely behind her own door does Maeve work out what the neighbour meant. This is Maeve, slapping her own forehead. Why. Why does she never. Get. It.

Me? I'm way past caring.

∅

Maeve cares. She can't stop.

Photo albums lie all over the floor. Nick piles them, one on top of the others like blocks. Whatever. As long as he's happy. A sip of tea and we're ready to go. Pick up the first one. Then another. We flip through the albums for a long time, page after page, finally settling on three pictures to set up on the windowsill. One, two, three. They lean against the glass. Behind them, the windows darken.

One. A photograph of my mother and Mahon, a long time ago, out on the coast where his Dad used to live. My father's on the front lawn with a cigarette between his fingers, and hair like bushfire. He's got tattoos where the blank white scars on his shoulders are now. Can't make them out. My mother hangs on his waist like a holster.

Two. The second photo, beside the first on the windowsill. Whatever the order, it's not chronological because this one shows

Mahon and Dave out behind their high school. Mahon looks at the camera. Dave half turns away. The boys aren't centred and the image is mostly of the tarmac behind them. A grassy crack runs from lower left to upper right. Their single shadow is almost as long.

Three. The last photo. Even older than the last. A teenage Mahon onstage. Junior high maybe. *Bat O he Ban,* reads the sagging banner behind him. His guitar's slung low. His hands are a blur, his mouth gapes, his tongue protrudes. He's not all there, my father. Vacant behind the eyes. Just like Nick.

Nick, who has made a stack of the albums, who stands on top of the sliding mass. Slips with rest. Alarm bells. Fire. Flood. Murder.

No, Nicky, no. False alarm. You're all right. Really, you are.

Tired. That's all. Ready for bed.

Ø

Ready for bed then. My mother finishes brushing her teeth. Stands in the bathroom, staring at her own reflection in the mirror. On her face? Nick's cat's-eyed, rhinestone bedecked, purple sunglasses.

A toothbrush cellophaned into its box. A new brush. A comb. A small travel toothpaste. A disposable camera.

Is that pee in that cup?

This can't be right.

LIGHT OF DAY.

Everything comes clear by the light of day, right? Everything has a place and there's a place for everything — just don't think too hard. Maeve sings in the kitchen. Nick eats peanut butter and toast at the little table. Gerbil curls in the belly. Gerbil rests — just for a moment, mind — beneath the steely curve of Maeve's ribs. My whale-mother. Swallow me whole. Change day to night. Let me play upon your rib cage, play and sing. Insides and outsides can be safely ignored while Gerbil rests, just for a moment, mind. Just for a moment while suns rise, float, streak night skies with their crazy setting. Chalk marks on blackboards. Pulls of a razor over inky scratchboard. Nice, clean lines and everything comes clear. Our lesson for the day. This day.

All right.

This day. Like the one before and the one before that, although I suppose I should admit I've been tuning in and tuning out, not following as close as I should. Lately, I find I prefer my feather bed to the tick-tock of my mother's clock. To hell with the logical, cogent flow of time. Overrated. Stale. Popping in and popping out — Gerbil-style. Don't you wish you could do the same, playing by my own rules in my capacious mansion, my house-of-houses? I don't like to give Maeve credit for much, but she's a damn fine bulwark. A really solid fortification against ... against ... To hell with the logical, cogent flow of time.

ø

Hey. Telephone. Surprise. Since when does my father call by the light of day? Carries with him the taint of the middle hours of the night. I hear the night wind as soon as Maeve picks up the phone.

— Where are you?

— *What?* shouts my static-voiced father. — We're in the van. Connection's not so great. How are you guys?

— Okay, hollers Maeve. — We saw the ...

Crackle, crackle, pop, says my father.

— What!?

— I said — *crackle, hiss* — went to the ...

— Great, that's — *hiss, hiss, crackle.*

Now suddenly the line is clear of static. The line is more than clear, the line is personal, familiar, tender — no cellphone of Dave's should be able to link my parents so intimately.

— Sweetheart. How do you feel?

— Pregnant.

— Old joke.

— We saw the doctor again. Everything's good.

— Good? You really feel good?

— I feel — what's wrong.

— Wrong? Why? Nothing's wrong.

— Your voice.

— Just the phone. Voices never sound right.

— But you're really on your way home?

A rush of surprise down here in Gerbil land, and I will admit to a case of the out-of-the-loop itch — a mild one, just a behind-my-knee-and-hard-to-scratch sort of case. Didn't my father just leave? Is the timing of his return to be just as fickle, just as sudden as his first appearance in our front hall? Oh, changeable Mahon. Oh, constant Maeve. My father arrives, settles in to stay, then vanishes up the phone. Only thing static about my father is the interference down the line — a crackle or two, Mahon breathing, the distant van's engine, and, behind that, the electromagnetic shadows of passing trees, the odd house. The warping of daylight.

— Mahon?

— That's the thing, Maeve, sez my father the voice. To my mother the body. The impregnable. Except, here's Mahon, buzzing in her ear like a well-aimed dart. Whistling words with feathers, a shaft, a sharp point. — Here's the thing. Dave booked one more. It's a chance to make a little more money before, y'know, before ... Maeve?

Maeve chooses not to answer. She leans her head against the hallway wall. Nick tugs at her shirt, saying, — Daddydaddydaddy.

— Shut up, she tells him.

— What?

— Sorry. Oh god, sorry, sorry.

— Sorry?

— Never mind.

— Never mind what, Maeve? I won't unless you think it's okay.

— Okay?

— Tell me the truth, Maeve. It's just that Dave's A&R guy....

— Oh, Mahon.

— I'll come home then. I'll ...

— You're right. We need the money.

— If I make some extra now I can — *crackle.*

— The line's breaking up.

— *Pop, hiss, crackle* — spend some time with Nick.

— Why would Nick need to spend time with you, Mahon? I'm here. I never go anywhere.

— *Crackle, hiss, pop?*

— What?

— *Hiss ... pop* — out of town.

— What if I asked you to come home?

— I'd come.

— Then tell Dave to turn around.

— What?

Maeve sits perfectly still, dry-eyed, watching Nick. I wouldn't be so silent. So passive. I'd be shouting, yelling into the telephone. Come home. Come home and face the music, mister.

— Dave wants to know if you're really asking.

— Well I'm kind of wondering what would happen.

Mahon translates for Dave, forgets to cover the mouth of the phone.

— Fuck that, says Dave. His voice is faint but not faint enough.

— He says if you wanted we'd turn around right now.

— I heard him.

Inky black. Daylight warps. What's an itch in the finger to all that night wind?

— I love ... *pop,* says my father.

— Yeah, says Maeve.

— *Hiss* ... I miss ... *hiss.*

— Yeah ... me too.

— I didn't catch ... *Buzz-zz-zt* ...

— *Hiss* ... call later ... *hiss* ...

— What?... *hiss.*

— I ...

— *Crackle,* says the phone.

— Mahon?

But now the phone won't say anything at all. Leaves Maeve squatting in the hallway in the perfectly pointless light of day.

Ø

A witch has crawled up our stairs, knocked on our door— Maeve spies on her through her security peephole. This witch must know we're alone. Hear her bang again on the door with her crooked fingers, her blood-red talons. A witch. A nightmare. Don't open the door, Maeve. Don't let her in.

My mother opens the door, greets the witch politely. Seems to expect her. — Come on in.

The witch hunches her way into the living room and sits dead in the middle of the chesterfield. Lights a cigarette. Maeve shakes her head. Rolls her eyes. Won't provide an ashtray. The witch smiles crookedly, produces an ashtray of her own — a snap-open box with an enamel cover — from the bottom of her giant witchy-handbag.

— P-le-e-eze. You know it's not good for Nicky. Or the baby. It's not good for you.

— I'm addicted, Maeve, says the witch with a straight face.

— Can't help myself. Besides, you lived. You all lived.

Maeve opens a window. Cool air rolls in. A bit of spring.

Nick comes out from his hiding place between the bookshelf and the chesterfield. The witch's voice has been working away on his mind, has be-spelled him. But he comes armed with a deeper magic: her name. — G'amma, he calls, peeking out at her. — G'amma.

— Nicky. There he is. My good-looking grandson.

Getting hard to trust these family members who pop out from behind our hallway door. Gerbil grows tried of surprises, getting too old (by which I mean sophisticated, of course). Gerbil plays in her capacious mansion, making up her own rules, but c'mon. C'mon, c'mon. I don't need more of these familial lacuna; I've found holes enough in the past few days (weeks, years) for a Gerbil to fill with a twitching nose, to smell out, to crawl into maybe for a little nap.

No one cares. The witch, the grandmother, holds out her arms, ready to pull Nick into a hug. Nick allows himself to be drawn in, receives lipsticky kisses on his fair cheek, a warrior's wreath of smoke on his black head. Nick, you shit. Can't you see your mother needs you?

Maeve sits alone on a straight-backed chair directly across from her mother. Knee-to-knee they sit. Face-to-face. Eyeball-to-eyeball. Nick nestles next to his grandmother with his hands in her handbag. He's pulling things out like a magician's apprentice. Lining them up on the chesterfield beside him. Wallet. Lipstick tubes. Lighter (the grandmother's scratchy voice — Give that to me, Nick; that's not for you). Tiny pillbox (— Childproof. A rebellious look at Maeve). A sheaf of bills bundled together with a rubber band (— Uh-uh, leave it. Nick leaves it). A bright red apple (— Go ahead and eat it). Several stones of various shapes and sizes. Car keys. A sanguinary bottle of nail polish. Another set of keys. Pens. Pencils. A gold hoop earring (— So that's where it went). Objects pile up. Nick counts them.

— One. One. One ...

The witch bestows a crooked smile on her grandson, flashes it at her straight-backed daughter. — So smart, this Nicholas. Much smarter than you at that age.

Maeve says nothing. The witch stops smiling. Taps her cigarette into her ashtray. Looks her daughter in the eye. — I'm double parked, she says.

— And I'm having second thoughts, says Maeve. Second sight more like it. Terrible visions.

The witch wrinkles her nose. Shrugs in a way that's terribly familiar. In a way I don't want to contemplate. — No matter, Maeve, she says. — I had to come into town anyway. She stops. Pulls on her cigarette. Playfully takes a poke at Nick, who grabs her gory fingertip and giggles. Stones, keys, papers, bottles, and boxes tumble off the chesterfield and bounce off the floor.

— Oh, what the hell, says Maeve.

Then, without a proper transition, we're all in Nick's room. Haven't been in here in a while — least important room in the apartment in my humble estimation. A new piece of furniture catches my eye. Long. Flat. I can't help feeling a little surprised. Did the witch come with her own bier of thorns? — Look, G'amma, my stupid brother calls in an excited voice. Bounces up and down.

— Did you buy that new, says the witch to my mother. She raises one witchy eyebrow. My mother ignores her just the way I ignore Nick. Exactly the same way.

Maeve walks over to the crib that sits by the window. The window blind hangs, half-drawn against the day. Rays of light seep underneath, illuminating something folded on the crib's clean sheets. Maeve lifts it up. — Remember this? she says, holding the object out to the witch.

The witch takes the yellow cloth. — I gave this to Nick, she says. Then she does something I don't like. Holds it up to her crooked nose. Inhales. Breathes in again. (Where's her cigarette?

She doesn't have it now. Did she put it out? Must have put it out.) — Babies smell so good, she says to Maeve, and crooks that eyebrow again. Maeve nods. — Have to, says the witch, if they didn't, we'd kill them. Then the witch laughs. — Nature, Maeve, don't make such a face.

My mother takes the yellow bunting away from her mother, replaces it on the crib mattress. Moves over to Nick's dresser drawers. Picks up a sheet of paper and hands it over. — I've written everything out, says Maeve. — Where you'll find his diaper bag, his car seat — you have to take his car seat, mother, or I'll never speak to you again — what else? His Mousie. Don't forget that or you'll be truly sorry. When I ... When we get closer to ... I'll have a packed bag here on the dresser. Are you looking, Ma? Are you listening to me?

The witch is reading the sheet of paper that Maeve has given her. She sits on the long, low bed beside her grandson and closes her eyes.

— If this is too much, Ma ...

— 'Course not. Eyes snap open again.

— 'Cause I can ask ...

— When's he coming back?

Maeve doesn't answer at first. Rubs her forehead, sore from slapping. — There was a schedule ... doesn't matter now. Soon.

— Cutting it close.

— Nick was so late.

— Second one can come on plenty quick. You're all stretched out.

— Ma.

— Nature, Maeve.

— We've got time.

— Sure you do, love.

Ø

My mother kisses the witch at her door, watches her humping the handbag down the stairs. Nick stands on the top stair and waves vigorously. Loves that witch with all his heart. Wish I could too, big brother. Wish I could like her even a little. But I'm too busy watching Maeve, leaning on the doorframe. Sagging with worry.

Across the hall, Darcy opens her door. She's all dressed up to go out, this neighbour of ours. Digs in her purse for her keys. Looks startled to see Maeve standing there. Looks a question at us. — My mother, answers Maeve, waving her hand in the direction of the fading clunk-clunk of the witch's court-heeled shoes. She sighs, lifts her eyebrows. Blows her hair out of her eyes. — Sheesh.

Darcy looks confused for a moment, then brightens. — Family, she says at last, shaking her head. — Know all about that.

Sure you do, Darcy, with your skirted ass prancing past Maeve, blowing a kiss to Nick (oh so happy to be waving again). Tip-tapping down the stairs in your high-heeled shoes. Passing Nick's grandmother with a singsong 'hello' that carries all the way up the stairwell. What do you know about family, Darcy, as you mince out onto the damp pavement with your traitorous drawing pad under your arm? As you leave behind the mother of us all, the giant Maeve, pumpkin-round at the top of the stairs. Jack-o-lantern-faced. Scowling. The witch's daughter.

My mother.

Ø

The witch's daughter takes Nick to the library. Four painfully slow blocks in the rain. Nick won't ride in the stroller, wants to walk, to check out the sidewalk worms curling like hairless Gerbils. Motherless guts. Excretory systems. Rudimentary brains. Oh, remember the days?

Maeve takes the stroller anyway because she knows Nick won't want to walk those same blocks home. Besides, the stroller is useful for carrying home the books that my mother will never find time to read. Still, once she's at the library, the dripping wet stroller poses a number of problems. She can leave it folded in the entrance and risk it disappearing — not likely but a potential disaster with funds so short. She can push it into the library, earning irritated looks from staff and patrons alike. In the end, Nick decides her by rushing past and disappearing deep into the library. Maeve leaves the stroller, unfolded, in the entrance. Hopes it *will* disappear. Can't stand another second of this. Not. Another. Second.

A second later, she finds Nick in amongst the picture books. A wicker basket of board books sits temptingly beside a comfy scattering of cushions. Nick seizes the basket, lifts one end with a giant smile as his mother waddles into view. — No, Nicky, no, whispers Maeve as a cascade of books heralds her arrival. Oh god, haven't we been doing this for centuries, eons, since the birth of time? Haven't we done it enough?

Library patrons look around at the noise, frown. Maeve bends over (a trial in itself) and begins to pick up books. — Help, Nick, she tells my brother. — Put them back now. Nick throws books into the basket with vigour. — Nick. Stop. Please. Maeve abandons the book basket, wrangles Nick down an empty aisle. Children's non-fiction, this time. Against a backdrop of tall books on whales, short books on marine mammals, fat books on sharks, she reads Nick the riot act, hears the sound of her own voice and stops, suddenly so tired of all of it. — Go on, Nick, she says instead. — Enjoy yourself.

My brother wanders up and down the aisles of the children's section. Fiction, non-fiction, early readers, children's poetry, atlases, fairy tales, paperbacks, hardcovers — each a spine to grab hold of, push down on. A book to flip onto the library broadloom. A book for Maeve to retrieve, replace as best as she can before moving on to the next. Every now and again she picks up a book of interest, transfers it to the canvas bag she carries for the purpose. Then she's on to the next. And the next. And the next.

Between the top of a row of books and the bottom of the shelf above, Maeve sees another woman come into the library. The woman carries a baby and leads a toddler by the hand. Maeve has never seen this woman before. Crouching, she watches as the woman settles herself and her offspring on the comfy cushions by the basket of board books. Bored books. Selecting one of the most boring, the woman begins to read.

And that's all. Her children listen. The baby sleeps and the toddler snuggles. For an entire minute, they remain in the same spot. Then Maeve must move, following Nick into Children's Fiction, Hel to Mac. She spots the blessed family again through a gap in the row. Same position. No movement. Maeve straightens, stands amazed. Sights them over the low bookshelf, watches until they finish the six page board book. The mother gives the book to her toddler, who takes it carefully to the basket. Squats cutely, diapered bum in the air. Sets the book within the basket. Selects another and carries it carefully back to her mother.

Ho-lee. Maeve wants to whistle but her lips are too chapped. Besides, Nick has disappeared already, leaving behind him a trail of chapter books. Pages flap in the breeze he generates wherever he goes. Maeve half-turns to chase him when, to her horror, he reappears beyond the bookshelves, dead on target for the sainted threesome. Nick roars up, stops, stands staring a skinny foot away from the trio. Three round faces watch him, surprise working its mildest magic — an eyebrow considers lifting, lips part only slightly. Pulse rates hardly increase. Except for Nick's whose heart bangs the walls of his chest, a fist breaking free. Go. Nick goes, steps over the family and begins to decimate the shelves of picture books behind them. One in ten he drops with a thud. Thud. Thud.

Maeve arrives from stage right with her winter coat flapping. Swooping down on my brother, she scoops books from the floor. Shoves them back on the shelf. Wrests the next from between his fingers. Provokes screams of frustrated rage. — No, Mommy, no.

Nick straightens. Arches. Slides to the floor with howls and wails. Slippery in his purple snowsuit, undone all the way, he slides between her fingers, lies screaming upon the library broadloom. Oh, he's impossible. Uncontrollable. An oven-shaped millstone around my mother's neck, ready to drag her down to sleep with the fishes and the pasta jars and the flaccid underpants swimming in schools. He's a grey, flat blandscape that stretches on and on and on forever.

Except that Maeve understands the order of things much better than ever before. Watches her child writhe on the floor — watches him *LindaBlair* on the floor — possessed by nothing worse than a sense of himself. A certainty regarding what's his by right. Self-possession.

Watch Nick with something akin to respect. Let him rave on.

Ø

Here's how Nick's mother leaves the library, how she pulls off another remarkable exit. She gathers up her boy. He's finished his fit by now — dissolved his distress in a solution of rage. Maeve holds him, and he holds her, clinging tightly as he chokes and swallows down the tears of his righteousness. She sees anew the sweet-faced family watching from the comfy cushions. Accidentally, the eyes of the two women meet. Pale and alarmed, the good mother, with her children at her feet, seeks for something comforting to say, as if comfort were her business. Perhaps it is.

— He's tired, she tells Maeve. Best she can do.

— He's an asshole, Maeve tells her back. God's own truth. Maeve smiles in saintly certainty. Sails away with Nick in her arms. Pauses a second in the doorway to kick the stroller down the steps and then vanishes — a fade into the pencilled rain.

Ø

Good one, Maeve. That was a good one. Not all our moments are like that, certainly not. But how to keep them straight? Light of day. Keeps happening. Inky nights. Then light of day. Another inky night. How to line them up — soldiers of the international dateline? And to what possible end?

Maeve chooses to punctuate this new light of newer day with another visit to Darcy. Darcy-depraved. Darcy Depriver. I would warn Maeve again and again about her but she never listens. Never has. Won't now. And what can I do anyway? Not even the thought of Darcy's treachery goads me into movement in this dingy, cramped place. Only yesterday (or last week or last month — not sure and don't care) my surroundings seemed palatial, a liquid wonderland with pools and fountains and marbled courts. Now all I got is a crack in the wall only inches from my face. A trickle of dry plaster the only thing flowing now. I've got my knees in my mouth and gums 'round my knees. I wear my ceiling like a hat. Can't get the torque in here for a warning poke, a heedful slap. I could gouge, but seems I've lost the urge for even that. A depressed Gerbil, flattened by days, by nights. Squished into two dimensions by the same red wallpaper running underfoot and overhead, from right to left and left to right. That wallpaper — flock, baroque, worn bare, torn, ripped away wherever I can reach. I had a bed once, a fine four-poster. Now I snooze with splinters in my butt. No bed. No lamp. No hot pad. No chair. No chest of drawers. No rug. No window. No ceiling. No floor. No room.

Maeve gets Nick down for a nap, closes the door to his room, oh so softly. The world is *her* oyster. (And I'm her pearl: itchy-scratchy, covered in mucus, so very icky-precious.) Maeve's horizons extend all the way across the hall where she can indulge that itch in her finger that has nothing at all to do with me. Bastard itch. Worse than Nick.

Maeve creeps across the hall between the two apartments, leaving her door ajar in case Nick wakes. Knocks softly.

Knocks softly again (but not so softly).

Knocks hard.

Maeve knows Darcy is at home. Could hear her moving around in the kitchen not long ago. Can hear music now, seeping under the door. Maeve knocks one last c'mon-now-know-you're-in-there knock — what right has she to knock like that? Footsteps approach the door. Maybe Maeve has interrupted Darcy while working, but there's nothing Maeve would rather see. Darcy's pen laying down that sweet line. That familiar line. Jaw ...

Darcy's door opens. Not Darcy behind it though. Duncan looks out at Maeve.

Now this makes no sense. Maeve takes a step backward. Duncan smiles at her. Spreads out the fingers of both hands in a gesture of deaf-mute surprise. Maeve might as well be deaf and mute. And blind.

This is silly.

— You just missed her, says Duncan, as if his presence makes sense. — She only left a minute or so ago. Just gone to the ...

Maeve doesn't let him finish. In her confusion, she's been looking all around, everywhere except at Duncan's face. She's seen the door hinge (middle one), the strike plate for the deadbolt (directly opposite), the corner of Darcy's hall where the fire alarm lives. The floor of the apartment (needs to be swept — a piece of paper distracts her).

— Should be back soon.

Maeve looks up at Duncan. Alarm bells. Fire. Flood. Murder. Well, nothing like that. Only a moment's insight. A piece of paper lying amongst the dust, crumbs, grit.

— Excuse me, she says politely to Duncan. — I think you're standing on something of mine. She points down at Duncan's socks (grey wool, hole in one heel). Every bit the man whose floor has become a hot plate, he jumps aside. I know the feeling — these sudden residential renovations ...

Maeve stoops over and scoops up the paper on the floor. She holds the lost schedule — Mahon's schedule, dates on the left, place names on the right. No head slapping. We're way past head slapping. Maeve wants to slap something else.

— Where did you say I might find her?

Ø

All around us St. Clair hoots and hollers. The street looks its best on a bright day, but I can't stand the green and yellow awnings, the yellow and green beans in their wheeled bins outside the grocery store. Don't even want to think about the racks of print dresses for the street's old women. Or the darkened windows of the sports bars where I can only ever see the corner of a bar stool, the sunbeamed knee, the distant red of a neon sign. I know without looking that the wires hang overhead. That the brick buildings loom. That the glowing sky hovers only inches from our heads. Sometimes, in the summer, the street turns white, de-peoples, looks Chernobyl-ized by heat. But not today — the weather today draws people outside to walk and talk. Today the street is full of voices, accents, languages. I hear tongues but no words, hear a babel, a babble, a bubble. I hear everything, and nothing in particular.

She's running up our street, Maeve. She's turning the air around her blue. She's bouncing around dangerously and running. At the lights she has to stop. Leaning against the light post, she gasps for breath and rubs her fingers along aching stretch marks. The plaster and lath of her rib cage heave. Stars circle before her eyes, around her head — pencilled spirals, a halo of little birdies. Maeve makes a cartoon recovery, leaning against the light post, peering past the pounding.

— Are you all right, dear?

Someone bends into Maeve's face. She shifts planes, focuses on the foreground. A face sharpens, comes clear: another middle-aged woman, like so many others. Like her soon. — Are you all right?

Overhead, the 'walk' light illuminates. Maeve stands upright. — I'm good, she says. And she begins to run again.

∅

Maeve finds Darcy exactly where Duncan said she'd be: in the Italian greengrocer's up the street. She juggles a bunch of endives. Asparagus. A lemon. Maeve rushes up behind Darcy, confronts her with the flapping page. Shouts. — Why did you take it?

— Hi Maeve.

— Don't say you didn't. I found it on your floor.

Darcy laughs. — Crazy, is all she says.

— Leave him alone, Maeve shouts.

Darcy looks at the paper, now pinched between Maeve's fingers. The paper droops. Darcy frowns. — Let me see it.

— It's not yours. Maeve presses the paper to her chest, Mahon's writing next to her heart.

Darcy keeps her puzzled eye on the page. Suddenly her face changes. She smiles, laughs. Sets down her endives, her lemon, her asparagus. — Maeve, she says.

— No.

— Maeve, listen. That's your picture.

— It's my schedule.

— Your picture. You left it that day you came over. I put it on the table by the door. Your — what's it called? Electropop? Technosound? Something like that.

Maeve stares at Darcy. Now Darcy is the crazy one.

— Look at it.

Maeve peels the schedule away from her heart. Sees Mahon's hurried writing. Dates and places, all past now. Slanting blue pen. Two columns sloping down the page. And, from the other side, a dark square bleeding through. Inky black. Maeve turns the page over.

— My ultrasound.

Darcy snaps her fingers.

Ø

Maeve walks home. She turned her back on Darcy and left. Should have said sorry. Should have said oh my. Should have said I never. Said nothing instead. Now she walks home, seeing how events conspired, all those weeks ago. Turns pages. Looks at pictures. Mahon on the telephone. Dave spieling off dates. Gives Mahon the schedule, but Mahon has no paper. Grabs the nearest scrap and turns it over. Begins to write. Presses his pen into the verso, incises lines into my papery organs, my inky spine. Marks me forever.

Duncan waits in the shared hallway, both doors open. He's been keeping an ear out for Nick, as ordered. Steps to the top of the stairs as soon as he hears Maeve's tread on the lowest. Watches her rising, rising, headfirst, until she's there on the very top stair, looking at him.

— Did he wake up?

— What? No. What did you — ?

— Thank you. Maeve cuts Duncan off. Moves past him and over her own threshold. Sure enough the apartment snoozes on. Nick snoozes on.

— Maeve. Duncan still rocks on the balls of his feet, in his socks, in the hallway, waiting to talk to her.

— It's all right now, Maeve tells him. Owes him that much of an explanation at least.

— Maeve, Darcy, she's ...

She cuts Duncan off again. Begins the process of closing the heavy door. — Doesn't matter, she says through the rapidly thinning opening. — Not any more.

Ø

An inky night. Light of day. What's this?

Mahon. No sooner does he slip between sheets than he slips out again, the fibres rough against his long legs, scraping lightly along his smooth back. Mahon on the bed edge, scratching his head, scratching his balls. Yawning.

There's only a little light through the venetian blinds, just enough for Mahon to find his shorts on the dresser. His T-shirt wrinkled on the rug. Socks nestled in the drawer that squeaks. The old man knows enough to pull gently — easing the invisible rollers over the hidden guide rail. He applies pressure in one direction with a hand on the drawer pull, applies pressure in the other with a hand held flat against the wood. Avoids squeak. Uncorks the tip of his tongue from the corner of his mouth. Smiles softly in the yellow dawn.

Deftly done, Mahon. Like a ghost, you are.

Mahon skirts the foot of the bed. He lifts the venetian blind with one finger, squinting into the pink and gold steam of a St. Clair morning. He wears his new trail shoes — considers his options. Over to the reservoir to run beneath the concrete arches? Down the grassy path past crumpled bum blankets, empties, a stink like the seats of Dave's van? Or how about west, toward Old Mill? Follow the Humber as far as St. James, along the paths haunted by once and future brides. Around the rock garden where anyone with an itch in their finger could sit and sketch all the brides of a single summer's day. Ten. Twenty. One hundred brides in a single landscape, on a single spot yanked hard through viscous time. Mahon could make a list of brides every time he ran there — an inventory of brides to make Maeve laugh. And when he came home he could lie beside us on the bed, still sweating, listing all the brides on his fingers.

The fairy tale bride in the white gown. The bride in the black dress. The bride who wore red. The bride with twelve bridesmaids. The bride all alone. The bride whose page boy fell in the pond. The bride who ripped her dress on the rustic railing. The bride whose hat resembled a UFO. The bride who ran up the gravel path crying. The bride and her twin who was also a bride. The bride who called her photographer names. The bride in gloves to her elbows. The bride in the hip cast. The bride in a mini right up to here. The bride with her Rottweiler. The bride who danced. The bride who limped. The bride in the bushes smoking a joint. The bride who put the best man's hand up her skirt. The bride with three fathers. The bride in the jewelled crown. The bride and her bride. The bride in a hooped skirt. The bride in the sari. The bride who sang. The bride asleep. The bride who carried dandelions. The bride with the diamond in her tooth. The bride who was radiantly pregnant. The bride who winked at the passing jogger.

— Oh stop, Maeve tells him. — I don't believe that one.

— She did. She winked right at me.

— No, radiantly pregnant ... radiantly, my butt.

Mahon says nothing. The bed is empty.

Ø

Maeve holds the schedule in her hands, feels possessed. Locates Dave's cell phone number, the emergency number, scribbled in blue pen along the top of the sheet. My father left it there for her. A secret message after all. Without pausing to think, she dials. Light of day — phone switched on. Dave answers on the first ring. Speed takes the breath away. Didn't know getting to Mahon could be that easy — never guessed.

— Maeve. As always, a pleasure, Dave lies.

— Gimme Mahon.

— And it's *lovely* to speak with you also.

— Gimme Mahon.

— The magic word, Maeve. Even Nick ...

With an amplified clunk, the phone is taken away from Dave. My father answers, speaking eagerly. — Maeve?

— Come home.

— What?

— Come home.

— You mean, now?

— I mean for good.

WAKE UP. I WAKE UP. I DO.
Remember with what energy Gerbil woke up once upon a time? Sesame seed eyes bright and sharp under furry lids. A twitching nose. A slew of demands as long as my tail — blah, blah. Not this morning, no. Lately my words dribble. Feeling flakes, crumbles, dried to a dust. My own heart serves as a sponge to the tip of my tongue. Things I need to say vaporize before they ever reach my lips. Poof. Eyes brim, but tears evaporate. Spit dries. Gums crack.

Eyes stick. And I'm sliding back to sleep.

From far away down the hall I hear the quiet tug of the apartment door and the click of the deadbolt. Someone moves out there. With my supersonic hearing, I can hear Nick stirring under his Lion King sheets. I wait for him to rise, shine, shout. A moment later, Nick's shiftings and creakings subside. His stertorous breathing resumes. Nick sleeps again. And I gnash my teeth. How can he sleep when I want him cracking, smashing, screaming, thumping? Doesn't he know, I want him moving. Rouse the house now, Nick. I'll send confetti though your mother's belly button. I'll put my lips to her like to a mouthpiece, hooting her like a horn. I'd call your name soccer-style, leaning hard on the whole syllable of you. And if I had the room I'd hold my arms above my head, one hand congratulating the other.

Wake up, Nick. Wake *me* up. Wake up the Gerbil I used to be.

My house is gone, collapsed inward with me still inside. Caught in a human rock slide, crumbling mortar and wallboard, snapping two-by-fours. I'm rolled upside down, wedged in here with my feet waving in the air, except there's no waving. Each foot, every toe is packed in rubble, immobilized by fragments of shattered bladder, shards of stomach, gravelled brain from the clifftops. Imagine a fossil showing lace-like ribs, whiskery fault-lines, seed shaped formations peering from rock. You might

chapter ten

doubt this impossible object — a sort of Piltdown Gerbil, you think. Well, let me be the first to respond. Let me wake up and deliver an opinion. And I will — I'm working on it.

I know I heard someone in the hallway just now. Someone tugging on the apartment door. Someone turning the deadbolt. Someone leaving in the yellow dawn. In the pink and gold steam of a St. Clair morning. Wearing his trail shoes. Wears his ball cap now that watch cap weather is past. I know who he is. Long time since he surprised me.

Must have been a welcome home. Must have missed it. Must have been quite a sight. Nick flying at him from the door of his room. Chest to chest. Atom smashers. Knocked back on his heels, hugging Nick hard. — Home, he says, his lips in Nick's hair. And later, a glad smile for Maeve as he slips between sheets, the stubble on his chin rough, scraping lightly. Then, every morning, sitting on the bed edge, scratching his head, scratching his balls. Yawning. Getting ready for running. Tugging on the apartment door. Turning the deadbolt. Going out. Going in. Coming in. Coming home. Over and over and over again.

Coming home. Going out. Leaving me alone with this Sahara between my toes. Parched and shrivelled, my feet stick straight up. Why do my soles feel so dry? Why do they feel cold? Wake up, Gerbil. Wake up. A tide line of amniotic warmth ebbing, drops to ankles, to knees, bathes bare midriff in cold air. Upside down, my armpits are above my chin, above my nose, above my eyes. Will the water gurgle around my head as if down a plug-hole? Which way will it twist? Clockwise? Widdershins like in all good fairy stories? Don't know. My eyes feel like gravel, rolling in sockets. Wake up. Where's my morning tea? Where's my saline sea? Everything feels chalky to the touch, like my flaking fingers have been too long in bathwater. But rock fall crushed my bathtub. Pulverized debris floats upward, stains what little remains of the shower curtain. I was only riffing before. I was only fooling, and now my nose fills with powdered stone.

Ø

Maeve stands on the bathroom floor as stone crumbles on the tile between her bare feet. She's up now, wide awake and wondering if she's dreaming. Maeve stares at the little cloud of dust, the plume of powder that drifts toward her knee. Grave as an Easter Island head, she notes the rubble that freckles the tops of her toes. She touches her inner thigh with her finger, pulls it away as if sticky despite the dust that rims her nail. Grabs a towel from the hook on the back of the door and drops it on the tiles. She leans over, meaning to swish the towel back and forth to wipe the dust from the bathroom floor. Instead, she grunts, groans, checks inside her inner thighs again. Her short laugh embarrasses me, and she uses her foot to sweep the towel across the tiled floor. The white towel comes up rusty. Ochre.

— Mahon, she calls feebly, still wiping. — Mahon? She puts her hand on the wall and bends forward at the waist. — Oooo, she says, then calls Mahon a third time. A moment later Maeve straightens. Somehow, she's managed to get the towel up off the floor. Lumbering from foot to foot she strips off her underpants and tries to wring the two cloths together into the toilet. Dust floats upward, gets up my nose, makes me sneeze. — Uh-h-h, says Maeve suddenly, gripping the sink. She huffs, puffs at her bangs. Tries to blow me out. Her hand gropes for the doorknob, turning, her voice only so much wind down the hallway. — Mahon? Ma-ha-ha-hon? But Mahon fails to appear. Only Nick's voice forces its way into the hall with its street-fighting vowels, action-hero consonants. Imagine him, standing upright in his crib, Mousie tucked in his pyjama waist like a gun. Arms crossed. Ready for action.

— Shit, says Maeve to herself. To me.

Maeve bends at the waist, holding her dusty thighs, drops of ochre on the tile — that bloody rock gets everywhere. She leans into the doorknob, rocks on her feet, steps backward pulling the door after her. Nick begins to call, demanding to be sprung. Soundtrack to a jailbreak. Maeve sinks back to sit on the bath mat lying folded on the side of the tub. Ochre everywhere. Maeve clenches.

Mahon left the apartment. I know. Mahon rose. Shone. Went out into the yellow morning. Pink dawn. Blah, blah. There he goes, fully awake in the misty air. Breathing deeply. Easily. Sprinting off into the distance. He's so *fit*.

Maeve bleats his name. She's called him back to her by secret code, by cell phone, by demonic possession. She's called him — she *calls* him to help her. For this. For now. Her hands are on her concrete abdomen. A cement egg cracking under her skin. Maeve calls Mahon, but Nick calls her, hammering the rails of his crib with his fists.

God, I'm dry in here. Dusty. Parched. I get rubble in my mouth with every breath. Up my nose.

Maeve rises. The grimy bath mat joins the towel and the panties on the floor, laundry for later. Maeve faces the sink, turns on the tap, and sand pours from the faucet. Undeterred, she runs her hands together, leans over the basin, and flings grit in her face. Then she wipes her grimy face with the hand towel. Grabbing a clean towel from the shelf, she wads it between her legs, holding it in place with one hand while she waddles out of the bathroom and into the bedroom. Now she works as fast as she can, making good the minutes between dust storms, between earthquakes. Holding the awkward towel in place with one hand, she rummages with the other in the drawer for clean underwear, for the box of pads last seen nine months ago. Checks the bedroom for signs of Mahon, notices absences as usual: holes where his shoes should sit, where his hat should hang. My mother looks for her watch to time the landslides, the seismic rumblings, but has no time to waste searching for it under the clutter of the bedroom. No time for timing. She heads to Nick's room to stop the noise.

Lifting him from the crib almost kills her.

— Daddy? says Nick as soon as he hits the ground.

Maeve brushes past her first-born and makes again for the bedroom door. Counting. Thinking. Breathing. Planning. Grunting. She's got her suitcase on the end of the bed with its confusing contents: new bathrobe, toothbrush in its cellophaned box, purple sunglasses to make her smile. Nick follows her. Stands just inside the bedroom door. Breathes loudly through his nose.

A moment later Maeve stands in the hall and stares helplessly at the wall of her apartment. What does she hope to see? She rubs her eyes with her knuckles, dislodges a sprinkling of white dust that stains her cheeks and grinds under rotating knuckles. At the level of her belly, Nick struts in a circle around her, demands breakfast. Wants breakfast now. — Nick, Maeve says. — Quiet. Mommy needs to think.

Nick lowers his voice. Gets quiet-*er*. He whispers, — B'ek ... fast ... b'ek ... fast ... b'ek ... Maeve, in a sudden rage, roars, grunts, doubles over, making Nick stare. Making Nick burst into tears.

Now what?

Now nothing. Now we wait. Twiddle our thumbs if we can. Our toes if not. Wait for Maeve to straighten up as best she can, to lumber to the kitchen and slap together a peanut butter sandwich for Nick. — Mommy's in labour, she tells him, as she hands him orange juice in his drinking cup. — Um, says Nick, thinking, I'm sure, of dump trucks, girders to the skies, rough men in hard hats. He smiles. Mommy's a union organizer. Mommy's a teamster. Mommy's in labour. Oh good one, Nick. Nick smirks, eats peanut butter, drops the crust behind the radiator.

Meanwhile, Maeve labours. Shaken by land tremors, earthquakes, tsunamis of dust and debris, she transfers her suitcase to the hallway. Grunts. Groans. Catches her breath. Spies the phone and pulls it toward her and dials. Maeve waits, a ringing in our ears — a side effect of her condition or evidence of an empty room, who can tell? Certainly not me, not Gerbil, your narrator, whose ears are filled with the sound of falling rock. A chunk of granite lands on what little remains of my baby grand. Dissonant notes jangle, grind, tune themselves into the long beep. Maeve leaves a message.

— Ma. It's started. Oh shit. Whew. *Whew.* Hospital with Nick. Taxi, fastest. Mahon — well ... Mahon ...

Hanging up in slow motion, Maeve curls into a small boulder, a conglomeration of marbled bone and fleshy clay. Look. You can make out even the smallest pieces of her: tiny red coals that make up the shape of a woman. And deep at her core sits the glowing, molten visitor, shifting phase — red to yellow to full-spectrum heat. Maeve picks up the receiver again and manages to push six of the seven buttons that will call her a cab before she's driven into the dining room to beat her hand on the windowsill. But that's just her. Maeve moans. She rocks back and forth on her heels, hands spread wide on the radiator's spine, coming forward at last to lean her cold cheek on the glass. Whispering. — What will I do? What does she do? Looks out the window for Mahon and sees a familiar head in the street below. She pushes up the sash — finds the strength from somewhere — and calls wildly.

's not him. Not anyone we know. A complete stranger. Let's follow him — he's getting on the streetcar. Go along with him for a rattling ride. A storybook day. Warm and finely drawn. Down to The Beaches maybe. Past all those wood-sided houses, down along the boardwalk. All bright sun and big blobs of purple pigment. Deep blue. Pooling just so. A stretch of white paper for the right bit of beach. Finding it glittering and clean. Selecting a place. Roughing in the waves at the water's edge with the tip of the brush. Sun a warm wash. Clouds a wet squiggle. But what's this in my mouth? Sand. Grit. Forgot myself. Forgot myself. Won't do at all.

So damn thirsty. And then we go white, yellow, red, and, finally, the blissful black obsidian of cooled magma.

Maeve calls a cab, and the voice tells her there's a fifteen minute wait. She puts down the phone and goes to stand by her bag. She's scared that if she tells them to hurry — that she's having a baby — they won't come at all.

Thinking ahead, Maeve gets another towel from the bathroom, determined not to mess up the seats of the taxi. But Nick takes her towel and makes himself a bed on her suitcase. Then he changes his mind, wraps Mousie in the towel. Calls the bundle a present, gives it to his mother to open. But bad Maeve loses her temper and snatches the present from Nick, unfurls Mousie onto the floor, and places the towel between her soggy backside and her suitcase. Then she sits and evenly meets Nick's eye.

Nick frowns at his mother. Looks at Mousie on the floor. Looks back at his wicked parent on her bulging suitcase. Maeve shrugs and waits for the detonation. Nick, offended, crouches down, pokes at Mousie. Soon he will mottle with anger. Will soon be screaming. Same old drill. But Nick remains squatting, merely regarding Mousie with an expression of internal concentration. A minute or two later, when he rises and tugs ominously at his own diaper, Maeve moans softly. Another unwanted present.

Maeve reaches feebly for Nick's diaper. — No poop, insists Nick, way ahead of her. He looks shiftily from side to side — a one hundred percent poop criminal. But Maeve chooses to take him at his word. Easier that way. And Nick, smiling his victor's smile, selects a new toy from his toy box. A plastic dinosaur. — P'ay, he says.

— Mommy can't play right now.

— P'ay.

— Already paying, says Maeve.

Same old joke, not funny last time, not funny this time. Again and again, Nick sets 'em up and Maeve shoots 'em down. But nobody's laughing. Maeve's hand shoots out, lays hold of Nick's wrist with her granite fingers. Nick wriggles, startled by the one-handed grip she has on his arm. His whole mother hardened. Turned to rock. He twists, but she holds him firmly before her.

— Count with me, Nick. Be my special counter.

— Ow.

— C'mon, count with me. One ... two ... three ...

— Ouch, Mommy. Ouch.

— Four ... five ... You'll live, says Maeve, but lets him go. He dances away from her, careens backward into the edge of the living room door. Nick stops dead, feels carefully behind him until he finds the door jamb with his hand. He looks at Maeve, turns red. — Seven ... eight ... chants Maeve to herself. Nick's lip begins to quiver.

— Nine ... ten.... Jesus. Maeve gasps for air.

— P'ease.

— What?

— P'ease, p'ease.

— Oh, Nick. I don't know what you want.

— Mommy, *p'ease.*

Maeve puts her hand over her eyes, blocks out the sight of Nick. Breathes in. Breathes out. Breathes in and out. Nothing but her breath. Going in. Going out.

Thirst. Dying of it.

— I can't stay here, Maeve announces. She moves over to the window to check on the cab. The street below seems impossibly empty for this time of morning. A curve of concrete and tar, mildly post-apocalyptic. Nick climbs up beside her, points with a finger. — Outside? he asks archly. Maeve shakes her head. Suddenly and ferociously, he hugs her hard. — Mommy, he says for no reason at all. Oh granite Maeve likes that, yes she does. She crumbles and smiles, dabs dry eyes. Hugs Nick back. Nick takes advantage, tries to swing into her lap. — No, Nick. Oh, Nick. Maeve rises, sighing, unclasping Nick from around her neck. She crosses to the phone and pulls out the list of telephone numbers. Dave's lurks near the top. Maeve picks up the phone but then thinks better and puts it down again. A whiff of van — a mixture of beer and armpit. Nobody wants that. Nobody needs that.

The street remains a cab-free zone. Maeve lumbers back to her suitcase and stands staring at it. Picks up the bag. — Get your shoes on, Nick, she says.

Nick smiles roguishly. — Poopy, he counters, tugging the back of his pants. Maeve grimaces.

I see that grimace. Flat as I am. Crushed as I be. Even under my rock, I can draw her curved frown for myself. Pencil her eyes. One. Two. Check mark for a nose. Get the grimace on the page. Make the note.

Maeve sets down her suitcase and waddles to the bathroom where she finds only the empty package that last night held the final diaper. Looking around, she spies the side of Nick's diaper bag only just visible around the corner to the hall. The bag hangs on a hook in the hall, or at least it does until Maeve yanks it down, breaking the strap in the process. She pulls it open and upturns the contents on the floor. The diaper bag yields a tube of Vaseline, a box of wipes, a pair of plastic overpants, and no diapers. Maeve stands there in the hall holding the empty bag. The broken strap dangles at her knee. She stands for a good long time. Breathing. Grunting. Breathing. Thirsty.

At last Nick breaks the silence. — Poopy? he says cautiously, looking up into her face.

Maeve speaks. — Right. Moves back into action. The box of sanitary pads is easy to find again. Somehow she gets down on her knees and pulls down Nick's pyjama bottoms. Opening the sticky tabs, she removes the diaper with a single backward wiping motion.

— Ow, says Nick. Taking a sanitary napkin from her box, Maeve sticks it into the bottom of Nick's pyjamas. The wings trouble her for an instant, but she sticks them down each pyjama leg and begins to laugh. Nick, on the other hand, looks down into his pyjamas and screams. Stiff-armed he tries to keep his pyjama pants around his knees even as Maeve tries to pull them up. The harder she pulls, the harder she laughs.

Ø

Wake up. Wake up, Maeve.

Maeve's not dreaming. And she's not asleep. She lies exhausted with her eyes open. At last she gets up from the floor and does the thing she should have done long ago. She unbolts the apartment door and crosses the hall to Darcy's. She bangs so hard she hurts the heel of her hand. Darcy's boy answers and even in her current state Maeve sees the way his sleep-tousled hair falls in his face.

— Darce! calls Darcy's boy not taking his eyes off Maeve's face. — You better ...

Darcy appears behind him, suitably sleep-sodden. She wears a long-sleeved T-shirt that, judging by the size, is his not hers. Darcy lifts one sleeve-covered hand and pushes her short bangs out of her eyes. — You look like shit, she says, looking at Maeve. — What's he doing? With the other sleeve, she points at Nick, who lies in the hallway, heels planted, back arched. He's struggling to reach deep into his pyjama pants. Nick gropes. Grabs. Gives up and rolls out of his twisted pyjamas. He lies panting on the lino. Darcy calls him and he comes crawling to her, bare bottom and all. Darcy scoops him up. Maeve lets her. — Jesus, Maeve, what did you do?

— Me? says Maeve faintly. — Me? She laughs.

Nick shifts in Darcy's arms, turns to look her seriously in the eye. — I got no diaper on, he says, clearly but with effort.

— I can see that, Nick, says Darcy. — A bare ass is what you got. Don't pee on me, 'kay?

Nick nods.

Darcy's boy reappears, pulling on his shirt, kicking his shoes up the hall toward them, carrying something that jangles between his teeth. — Wha' 'ospi'al? he asks, talking through his car keys.

Ø

Saved. Darcy's boy owns a clapped out Toyota. He starts the engine. On comes his music, cranked to shake the neighbourhood awake. Next, he climbs out of the driver's seat, takes Maeve's hand, leads her to the shaking car. He lowers her under the door frame with a careful hand on the back of her head, just like a cop. Maeve tries to sit on her towel, but Darcy, climbing in by the other door, takes it away from her and puts it under diaper-free Nick instead, belting him in as best she can. The car seat has been left behind: no hooks in the Toyota, and no time to install them. Maeve swallows hard, gulps the guilt down somehow.

At the last moment, Maeve remembers Mahon. She's got a pen in her purse, but she groans for paper. Darcy and her boy hunt in the Toyota's dash, in their own pockets, find a little square of paper at last. Maeve writes Mahon a quick note, and Darcy's boy runs it inside.

When my father gets home sometime soon, he'll find the note stuck with a blob of spit to the apartment door. His only clue to whereabouts of wife and child — the name of the hospital and nothing more, written on a tissue square of Darcy's boy's best rolling-paper.

Ø

A right onto St. Clair. The Toyota's tires squeal. The speakers boom.

— What's your name, Maeve yells to the Toyota's driver. She's made a few guesses. Cisco Kid. Floyd. Childe Harolde.

— My name, he says, is Giovanni Giuseppe Vincenzo Boldini.

— At home they call him Joe. That's Darcy, calling from the other seat. — Everywhere else, he's Jay.

— For the letter. Only spelled, you know, like, J-a-y. But I'm thinking of changing it. I want a cooler name.

— Like what? Maeve straightens up. Feels almost normal.

A long silence settles over the Toyota.

Ø

Another right at the lights. A left. A right and a missed exit.

— I'm not coping. Now Maeve shouts in the bouncing Toyota.

— What? calls Darcy, looks to see Maeve clenched in her seat. Darcy winks at Nick.

— Not. Coping.

Jay hunches over the Toyota's wheel. Presses his runner to the acceleration pedal. Goes left. Goes left again. Wakes up a street of condos with bone-jarring sub-bass. The car doubles back and picks up the exit this time.

Darcy checks with Maeve. — Coping yet?

— Shut the fuck up, bawls Maeve. She means it.

Ø

C'mon, Maeve. Get with it. Wake up. We're almost at the hospital now and you know what that's like. First comes triage. You have to wait until they have room. There's always another couple sitting in chairs. Just sitting, unless the woman just sits *and* pats her abdomen contentedly. Contentedly? What the hell are they doing here?

Not. Not. Coping.

In triage, the nurse sticks her fingers between everybody's legs. But for some reason, I can't imagine her hand appearing in my field of vision. Never mind, when the time comes, Maeve, I'll see it for sure. I'm Gerbil. The nurse will wave; I'll wave back. Then ... um ...

Wake up Maeve. Wake — no, I said that already. Triage? Did I get to that part? Yeah, yeah. I'm warning — I'm warning *you,* Maeve. In triage, there's a long line stretching out past the door. A line of pregnant ladies from there to here. Everyone is patting tummies. Patting tummies, rubbing heads. Walking, chewing gum. Left foot in. Left foot out. The nurse waves from the head of the line. Maeve waves back. Darcy and her boy, Jay, dance in the street.

Not. Coping.

I'm ... I'm having a few technical difficulties. Words like little pebbles trickling down my throat. Coming back up again in an explosion of tiny stones. A spray of gravel.

In triage, the nurse sticks her fingers between everybody's legs, shouts, Get this child a diaper. *Stat.*

A glimpse of Darcy feeding Nick chips from a vending machine. She feeds him nachos and tries to teach him Rock-Paper-Scissors. Darcy makes a fist and counts one, two, three. And then there's Nick counting one, one, one ... Old joke. Lost on the nurse who rotates her wrist, checking her watch. Counts. Twenty-seven ... Twenty-eight ... Are we in the hospital yet? When Nurse speaks, her voice has changed. What did she sound like before? More cheery, not so urgent. — You might as well go straight to the delivery room, she tells Maeve, handing her two hospital gowns. — One for the front and one for the back. Keep your socks on. It's cold.

Handfuls of gravel smack walls. Rattle on windows.

Ø

I am a stone, set inside a stone. I always was an encrustation, but the passage from sedimentary to igneous crushes. A paralysis from toes, past knees, through groin, to waist, up chest, over shoulders, to jaw, eyes, until the whole of Gerbil goes solid. Maeve finally feels me, churning like a stone in the gizzard, a gastrolith rotating slowly. Unwilling partners, we chew over everything we share.

Ø

We share Mahon, far from here, standing before our battered front door. He lifts the rolling paper from the door where it's stuck. Parses the thin line of text. Then he brings it to his nose and sniffs. The scent of Thai-stick clings faintly to the paper. Admires Maeve's handwriting. The decided slope of her consonants. The sexy curve of her vowels.

Ø

Here's yet another damn surprise. We share Darcy, who sits where my father ought to be. Darcy pulls her chair near Maeve's head. The look on her face tells us she wants to be as far away as possible from Maeve's other end where the nurse applies pads as big and square as a sheet of drawing paper. With practiced latex fingers, the nurse rolls up the old ones and takes them away, covered in dust.

Darcy neglects to take hold of Maeve's hand. She neglects to wipe her brow with a face cloth. She forgets to whisper in Maeve's ear, telling her everything will be all right. Pale as marble is Darcy, and sitting so still you'd think she was the one turned to stone. Maeve looks up at her from her crumpled, kicked-in-the-gut position. —'s okay, Maeve tells her. 's awright.

Ø

We share Jay who sits in the tiny waiting area and waits. He and Nick wait together, hands between knees, heads hung. We share Nick, who peeks, adjusts his pose.

Ø

We share this story, a moon rock escaped from the museum, rolling downhill toward a glass town. This story has an unearthly genesis but develops a mundane momentum of its own. This story slips beyond a Gerbil's control. A grinding, a grating, a crushing. A stone rolling. An avalanche.

I can hardly speak. I can't speak. My tongue touches the corners of my lips, finds dust, finds more dryness. My voice cracks, grows gravelled. Turns sepulchral. As grave as stone.

This story grows too heavy. I'd like to crack this tale — one last joke. A bit of frozen water in a fault line, expanding, blowing the whole damn thing wide open. A liquid gag. A juicy punchline.

Witticisms dripping from a Gerbil's lips, drolleries running down my chin.

Thirsty.

Ø

— Fuck, she says, Fuckitty fuck! Take that fucking thing the fuck off of me.

Maeve sits up in her delivery bed now, the blanket slipping from her shoulder to reveal the green of her hospital gown. The cord of the fetal monitor catches beneath the folds of her rucked up gown, and she tears at it ineffectually, her fingers thick and clumsy, her eyes unfocused. The delivery nurse, beaming approval, removes the monitor. She reassures Maeve with a hand on her shoulder, with a smile. As the cord trails across Maeve's belly, she thrashes at it one last time, then settles back to gaze at the petrified Darcy. Maeve reaches out, takes Darcy's hand and puts the fingertips in her mouth. Darcy stiffens as Maeve bites. Hard. Darcy stifles a cry, too frightened of Maeve to say a word.

The nurse shuts off the fetal monitor. The absence of its electric hum, unnoticed until now, threatens to bring the walls down around us. Maeve spits out Darcy's fingers, luckily still attached to Darcy's hand. Darcy grasps them, wipes tips and palm on the overhanging fringe of Maeve's blanket.

Maeve pants. Breathes in. Breathes out. Her bag sits on a chair in the corner. Housecoat forgotten. Tennis balls in an old nylon forgotten. Toothbrush in its cellophaned box forgotten. Purple cat's ...

— Darcy. Do me a favour.

Maeve feels more comfortable now as the contraction diminishes, directs Darcy to her bag, to the pocket on the side where Nick's gift lurks. Maeve puts on the sunglasses, smoothes the blankets over her belly.

Breathe in. Breathe out.

Maeve sits in the bed, hands folded. She smiles at Darcy. Darcy gives Maeve what she's got: a tentative grin. But like a werewolf under the full moon Maeve begins to change, begins to crumple, to pant, begins to scowl. Not trustworthy, this Maeve.

Darcy rushes from the room.

Ø

My father supposes he should get a taxi but he has no money and no keys to his apartment. He stands on the sidewalk and gazes upward at his own windows, shining blackboards in the sky. As he looks, Maeve fails to sketch her own outline onto the surface, even though she always has before. This time she refuses to appear as the usual armature of lines that will shake its head, understand his plight, and toss him down his wallet. Irritated, my father scratches his beard, which makes him notice the roughness under his fingers, which makes him grumpy. He thinks of shaving his beard, his head. Of shaving his eyebrows, his legs, his balls. A hairless man fit only for a moon-launch or a diving bell in the depths of the sea. Any place other than here on this sidewalk, coinless, keyless. Clueless. Slowly now, my father begins to run in the direction of the hospital.

Draw me a series of panels. In each, he's smaller. In the last, he's gone.

Ø

In the waiting area, Darcy finds Jay, sitting in a chair. Just sitting there. Darcy tells Jay he needs to get up. Needs to take her home. She waves her finger in the air as she speaks. That Maeve, she's crazy. Sure she told Duncan she'd keep an eye on them. Sure she knows he loves his friends. But that Maeve. She's in there now. Just inside that dark doorway.

And as Darcy speaks, the tip of her finger waves, sketches the doorway. Draws Maeve waiting inside. Draws Maeve demonically possessed, wearing purple-rimmed sunglasses. Fills in what

Maeve said. What she did. Jay listens, watches for as long as he can. Then he holds his own finger up to his lips. — Shhh, he says.

— Shhh, yourself. Bitch bit me. She bit me.

Jay smiles, gestures. He shows Darcy Nick, who sleeps in the curve of Jay's arm, an egg in a nest. Jay strokes Nick's soft head.

— Oh damn, says Darcy. Sits down.

Ø

Nick stirs in his sleep, passed gently from arm to arm. He twitches suddenly like a dog dreaming of rabbits, dreaming of hunting, dreaming of running, but that's not what Nick dreams.

Nick dreams that Mahon runs. Really runs because he knows now that his earlier run was only a warm-up for this — the best run of his life. He's running faster than before, tempo but not quite race pace. Technically, he's running fartlek, speeding up and slowing down in tune with some secret wisdom of foot and heart. The word makes him smile as he runs; he even farts some, although there's no connection. He feels strong and able from the waist up, loose and relaxed from the waist down. People turn as he streaks by, his shirt flapping in the breeze. In a while, he'll take it off and then they'll turn to watch his slick shoulders, his pumping upper arms. It's getting hot. Soon he'll need to drink. But for now he's unstoppable, dodging strollers and seniors on the sidewalk, taking to the street to run even faster, seeking out the few green spaces, the leafy boulevards down which to run. He can't believe how far he's come. He checks his watch, presses the lap button just to hear it beep. Mahon kicks up his heels, runs faster.

Ø

— Nurse, calls Maeve, her voice imperious. Nurse. Nurse. Darcy. Mahon? Maeve adjusts the blanket over her shoulders. Draw her sitting up but make her rock from the waist down — painful, quickening, hardening, veined stone, full of strong blacks, speckled greys. Draw a slab of granite, thawing and freezing. And over her head, in a cartouche, carved names. Mahon? Nurse? Darcy!

Someone comes in from hallway, but it's neither Darcy nor Nurse. The arrival might be Mahon, but the vectors of the grin, strange fingers on the bar of her bed tell another story. — Darcy won't come, Jay says. — Won't come back in. She's watching Nick. There's only me. I done all kinds of stuff, but I never helped anyone ever get born before.

Maeve lifts her hand out from under the covers, crooks her index finger. Over their heads another cartouche: Giovanni Giuseppe Vincenzo Boldini, the time is now. She puts her hand on his sleeve, pulls him closer. Whispers in his ear. Tells him all about the architectural drawings she's making. Tearing them up just as fast. Arches shredded. Columns rip, crumble. Stone stairways collapse in tides of confetti. Not a grey wind but papery breath blowing. Windows, like pupils dwindling. A tail trailing, trickling down stairs, around corners, avoiding rock fall by a hair's breadth. Something living amongst the standing stones. An inky ghost in the pages.

Maeve stops speaking, gestures for water. Jay takes up a glass by the bed. The water slides, grain by grain, from the glass to Maeve's mouth. She swallows the dryness, gags. Coughs. A cloud of water from her lips billows, floats, settles to the hospital floor — a layer of red dust on the back of Jay's hands. Jay holds up his hand to the light, tests the grittiness with thumb and forefinger, stares at Maeve amazed. This is magic. Maeve moans for more water. But Jay drinks the last of it himself, eager to discover the trick.

— How? he asks Maeve, but Maeve sits upright and coughs driveway-sized gravel into a kidney-shaped metal bowl.

— Mahon, calls Maeve, rolling eye-whites to Jay who sees more stone there, opaque river pebbles between lashed shores. He touches Maeve's belly with the flat of his hand. Rock. He moves his hand to her breast — rock there too, a hard outcropping on either side of the breastbone. Maeve opens eyes, obsidian pupils inset.

Draw a stone creature from top to toe. A statue of a Gerbil. A rodent-faced sphinx buried in the sand. Capstones crumble. Extremities weather. A giant gerbil in stone like Ozymandias, with its head between toes. Toes between eyes. Eyes, jet pupils inset. Jade. Lapis lazuli. A gem of a Gerbil. Hard as diamond. Good as gold. This story is lapidary. This story is rock solid. This story is almost done.

Ø

Outside, in the waiting area, Darcy paces with Nick in her arms. Over the nurses' heads, the clock pops a coil, ceases to tick, grinds to a halt. Those nurses never even notice. Darcy helps those who help themselves. — Hey ... hey, what time is it? she demands, giving them a reason to look upward, to notice that time stands still. But they don't catch on, only change faces like they change shifts, substituting one for another by roster.

Nick wakes and takes Darcy to the basement cafeteria — the nachos have worn off and Nick's hungry again. The Lunch Special sign catches her off guard. — Is it lunch time? she asks the tired looking cook behind the counter. — Swedish Meatballs or Salisbury Steak? says the cook, waving a crusty spoon. Darcy puts back the mini box of Corn Flakes she'd chosen for Nick and orders him grilled cheese instead. For an instant, the day runs around her — rippled light from the glass sandwich-case flows like sand across the wall behind the cook, slipping over his ear, his cheekbone, his chin. Darcy turns and stares reproachfully at the dusty silk flowers, at the framed prints from the gift shop.

The illumination overhead falls flat and green.

Ø

Somewhere, several floors above, the nurse re-enters the labour room, asks are you man? Jay thinks, nods. Yes, he is. He's a little out of his depth. The nurse's hands move expertly over Maeve's marbled belly, slip under the hospital gown. The doctor enters the room now, hides her long red fingernails under prophylactic latex. In quiet voices, the women speak together of centimetres and degrees of dilation. Together they bend down between Maeve's legs, and Jay knows they're making careful study of the beginnings of things. The doctor taps experimentally with her rubberized nail, a gentle knock-knocking on heaven's door. It's a summons and everyone in the room holds their breath.

Ø

The pencil flies, roughing in shapes. Circles in frames at first, filling in the ground. Ghost lines marking horizons, measuring angles. Truncating cubes. Bisecting spheres. Then darker. A little more pressure. Etching the shapes with greater certainty. Outlining with a fluid plasticity. Scoring curves and contours. Foreground. Background. The whole: a template thirsting for the pen. The ink.

Ø

Giovanni Giuseppe Vincenzo Boldini, called Jay, counts in a flat voice. He's made a bad bargain and he knows it. He's hungry, missing lunch. He's missing the green daylight. He's missing testing the new speakers in his car, rolling up and down St. Clair watching shop windows vibrate. He's missing work. Who would have thought that watching someone get born would be so boring?

Jay counts to ten, counts to ten again, counts to seven, loses interest, loses count, starts on the alphabet.

— Keep counting, calls the doctor, scowling in Jay's direction.

— You want me to count? says Jay.

— Count, says the nurse.

— One ... two ... three ... From the bed, Maeve breathes hard, pants. While Jay counts, she draws her knees up as far as she can and pushes. She rolls her eyes. Jay feels her gaze sweep right through him, feels himself hanging, transparent and unseen, a ghost beneath the fluorescent lights. He stops counting; she stops pushing.

The doctor cries. — Man!

— I have a name, says Jay.

— Count, says the nurse.

Jay sits up straight. Counts. — Uno ... Dos ...

Ø

Breathe in. Breathe out. Pencil a line out the door, down the hall, past Darcy and Nick back from lunch, down the stairs, through the hospital lobby, down the worn stone steps. At the bottom of those stairs, draw a runner in recovery. Draw a man bent over, hands on knees, trying to catch his breath. The man lifts his head, gazes up, up at the building before him. Breathing in. Breathing out. He's run a fair distance and has only a little way left to go.

Mahon straightens and enters the hospital, wiping sweat from his brow. The two women behind the information desk see his flushed face, his still laboured breathing, look him over, wondering, perhaps, if he'd be better off in emergency. But he's ambulatory, nothing more serious than a wife in labour and a rush to get here. The women smile with pleasure, call out the floor number, point out the correct elevator. But Mahon wants the stairs. The women practically cheer him on as he leaps for that bottom stair, aiming for the finish line.

Ø

Darcy's telling Nick the best stories she knows — tells him which clubs, which after-hours, which speakeasies, which warehouse parties he'd like the best. Nick listens and pleases Darcy. Nick pleases Darcy so much that when she realizes the slick back and T-shirted head at the nurses' station belong to Nick's Daddy, she frowns, holds on to Nick. — Hey, Nick, she says. But Nick's already sprinting into an easy reunion — father and son. Hearts and sweaty flowers.

Ø

Maeve, wracked by confessions, takes off her sunglasses. Takes hold of Jay's shirt sleeve. — Don't bite me, says Jay.

— I'm sorry, Maeve says in a whisper so that neither the doctor nor the nurse can hear. They're in the corner with the gynecologist, quarrelling about a pre-emptive surgical strike.

— Wha — ? says Jay, struggling. — My mama had seven, he tells her. They both know that's not the point.

— Had to happen.

— Sure. It had to happen, says Jay, who hasn't a clue.

— I'm sorry, she says.

— Don't be, says Jay, speaking out of turn, but he's interrupted by a long, gut-centred moan from Maeve. Up come her knees, and the doctors, on instinct, swivel like a chorus line, soft-shoe toward her.

Comes another knock-knocking. Comes another summons for Gerbil.

Ø

Draw up Maeve's knees, pointing to a hospital ceiling. Draw her doubled over, peeling back, exposing pale Gerbil shamelessly.

But.

Ø

I have an architecture of my own — chambers of the heart, vascular hallways, a kidney-shaped pool. I *am* an architecture of my own — a stone heart, ribs like vaulting, windows that blink. Roofs that sag, floors that rot, walls that heave and pant. I'm a house, a red room, with something tailed that gnaws. Something with sharp teeth and inky eyes. With a taste for the tender bits. Something that chews over facts, leaves holes behind. The circular score of biting teeth. The straight score of a pencil lead.

Check for insides. For outsides.

Ø

Outside, the baby is born in a gush of liquid. No dust. A different kind of magic, Jay.

Mahon, drawn by the sound of cries, by the unmistakable mew of a newborn, comes running. Speaks the truth before anyone else. — Jeez, Maeve, he says. — *Another* one. Mahon stares at the wriggling baby boy in the doctor's arms. But he's laughing.

Maeve sobs, hiding her face behind her hands. Floods. Taps back on. Mahon rubs her shoulders. Tells her everything's okay. You're okay. Baby's okay. Maeve laughs, sobs, hiccups. — I know, I know, she says. — Only, I thought she would be someone else. She says.

Ø

Me too, Maeve. Imagine my surprise. How I feel. You. Me. We're all mixed up, my mother.

Nothing to do but pencil the ending together, fading up from graphite grey. Rough in a crib by the window, white bars taking heavy shadows. Lay down a sheet of acid-free paper with a different body nestling underneath. Different fingers. Different toes. Pick up a pen with a 0.3 mm line width. Draw a drawer full of different clothes, and some of Nick's hand-me-downs too. And in several years, draw a scatter of Lego bricks spreading from wall to wall, but with a different head bent down beside Nick's dark one. Draw a tidier bedroom, with neater shelves. Up on the shelves, draw a stuffed creature beside Nick's Mousie. Can anyone name that creature, so worn with love? Not a rabbit, the ears too small. Not a mouse, the nose is much bigger. Roman nosed, prick-eared, a crook in the tail. Not a usual toy — a different toy for someone else. Given perhaps for a different birthday (on the same day of the same month), with balloons and cake and friends from school.

Draw it all. Get it all on paper.

Tear it up. Throw it away.

Put your pencil down.

CHECK FOR OUTSIDES. FOR INSIDES.

Inside, I'm all eaten alive. Eaten inside out. Hollow. Parched. Thirsty for so long. But Nick comes and stands beside the bed. Checks out his baby brother in my arms, and I have to say something.

Well, I do.

I have a lot to tell them.

epiløgue

Ø

I would like to thank the faculty and students of the University of Calgary creative writing course who served as enthusiastic and thoughtful first readers so many years ago when this book was still a baby. Thanks to Aritha van Herk and, especially, to Nicole Markotić for providing coffee that wasn't coffee and kicks that weren't kicks — everything Nicole did was well-aimed and much appreciated. Thanks also to Suzette Mayr, from whose editorial advice I have learned so much.

Ø

Finally, I would like to thank my family for providing endless inspiration, but who are NOT the people in this book.

Ø

D. M. Bryan was raised in Edmonton, Alberta, where she liked to play dinosaurs in her backyard with the boy from across the alley — until he moved away when they were both four. She remained alone in Edmonton until adolescence when she moved to Calgary, where fate reunited her and her childhood playmate. Taken with this coincidence, they married, moved to Toronto, and produced a son and daughter.

Ø

Bryan has acquired an assortment of degrees over the years, including a BFA in Photography and an MA in Communications, both from the University of Calgary, and a BFA in Film from Ryerson University. After what she describes as "various yo-yo throws" across the country, Bryan has finally re-settled in Calgary where she now teaches sessionally at the University of Calgary. *Gerbil Mother* is her first novel.

The text is set in Scala Serif and Scala Sans, two neohumanist typefaces designed by Martin Majoor in 1991 and 1994, respectively.

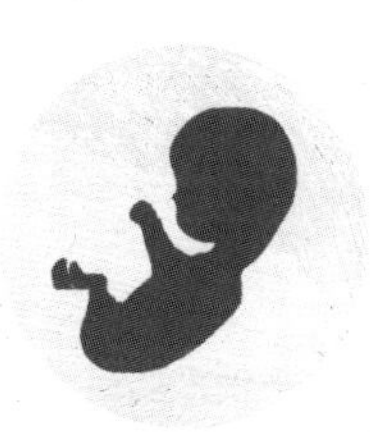